I0519654

BETTY'S ETERNITY'S DINER

WRITTEN BY KEITH STARBLUE

Betty's Eternity's Diner
(Pages 03-201)

(Extra Betty Short Story)
Betty Helps Misty Find Her Missing Ring
(Pages 202-217)

Copyright 2019 by Keith Starblue

ISBN-13: 978-0-578-49399-2 (Keith Starblue)

ISBN-10: 0-578-49399-3

Because of some mature themes presented within, reader discretion is advised.

Contact me at keithstarblue@twc.com

Betty's Eternity's Diner

Betty's Eternity's Diner
Chapter One:

(June 1st 1969, Inside a record shop in New York City.)

"Come on Richie, decide already, I'm hungry. The Beatles or The Stones you can't go wrong with either," Betty says impatiently, while rubbing the ends of her long brown hair.

"Peace Baby, I've got a bad trip going on in my mind and only the best of Rock and Roll can slate it and put me in a love groove, that will light up my karma like a rainbow."

"That was deep Richie, but it's probably that sack of bunk that you smoked. I told you not to buy it from him. I try to be polite and kind but that dude looked like he was born on Mars. I don't think that was even real grass."

"Wow, what a way to love thy neighbor."

"Well kiss my mean fanny, I'm leaving. I'm going to find a nice little place to set my tired bones down. Today we drove all over the place trying to find some grass."

"And we found it, didn't we?"

"No you found bunk from Mars. And then what did you do? You rolled it all up into four giant joints and passed them around to whomever stopped by for a toke or ten."

"I'm generous like that Betty. I give it away now then later I receive it back. Pure karma at its finest."

"Well Mister Cosmic Man, what does your karma tell you about what happened next?"

"What happened next, I forget?"

"Are you fried out or something Richie? You don't remember?"

3

"That's me baby, I'm all this way one moment then the next moment I'm on to something else. Living and being this way as a free thinking man makes it hard on the memory to remember the non-important."

"Non-important, really?"

"What can I say?"

"Well how about this Mister It's Not Important To Me, you and I running our butts off?"

"Oh yeah, that was funny."

"Funny? It was not funny when the two police men came walking down the sidewalk and yelled freeze, you pot smoking, long haired, hippy pigs."

"Well what do you expect from the police, they're never polite to ones like us. They hate us. In our 1984 there will be no more hateful police. They will be replaced by robots with great manners and sympathy for humanity."

"Robots? You wacko! I'm leaving."

Betty turns around and takes seven steps away from Richie and then she spins back around with the look on her face that she has something very important to say, "Richie, you I understand. I love you but you do look like a hippie p... What about me?"

"What about you Betty?"

"I'll tell you what about me. Look at me, I look nothing like a hippie pig. I'm the good looking girl from next door you fall in love with. Those mean police men hurt my feelings calling me a hippie pig, like I was a guy and not a innocent nice, lady."

"Betty you are the one that told me to find some grass

4

because you wanted to get high 'cause you were feeling low. It was your money and your car I used to find your grass for you."

"You didn't find grass, you found bunk, then we even lost that because we had to leave it behind so we could out run the police. How long do you think we still have to wait before we can go back to my car?"

"Not me Betty, forget your car, it's a lost cause."

"Well thanks for the great day Richie. Hades will become a paradise before I call on you again, you-you, you ass!"

Betty walks away shaking herself for the world to stop and watch as she goes walking by. Richie looks at the records in his hands and remembers that Betty was going to buy them for him because he has no money.

Richie says out loud for all in the record shop to hear. "This is not fair. The only reason I agreed to find her, her weed was because she promised she would buy me some new records. I went through all that and now I get no new records. No, this ain't fair."

With anger Richie with records in hand walks up the counter and tells the owner this, "Hey man, there's been a mistake made. That lady that was with me, well she was suppose to pay for these records. So if you want your money for them you better chase her down to get it. Peace and good day to you."

The record store owner looks confused at first until Richie walks out his shop's door with records in hand that he did not pay for, then the record store owner looks very mad indeed, "Hey you hippie, get back over here with those records."

The record store owner whose name is Joe runs around his counter and straight out the door to chase down Richie,

5

who now is running his tail off, sandals and all, "Go after Betty man, she has the money for your records," Richie yells out to Joe in a panic.

"You stinking hippie, give me back my records."

Richie who is still tired from running earlier, begins to realize that he will not be able to out run Joe. So Richie decides to toss the records on the sidewalk in hopes that Joe will stop to pick them back up.

"You hippie pig, you just destroyed my records. This is going to cost you."

"Leave me alone, you record store owner pig. Leave me alone, stop chasing me or I'll..."

Unfortunately for Richie when he turns back around to watch where he's running to he runs straight into the two police men that were chasing him earlier. Richie looks at the two police men and says, "Ah man."

The two police men, one older, one younger, look at the other and smile. The older one of course does most of the talking, "Well what do we have here Bentley?"

"I don't know Cargo but whatever it is, it surely stinks. Kinda similar to that of the stink of a pig."

"You are correct Bentley. This sorry excuse for a human being is what we polite society refer to as a lousy stinking hippie pig."

Richie can't help himself, "This ain't right. I'm a human being no matter what I look like to you. Who are you to judge me for who I am or what I look like? I can tell you this, I'm a really great person that loves life, peace and liberty. By the way I'm not the pig, no you two are the pigs. I'm sorry you made me tell you this."

Joe, who just about caught up to Richie before he ran into the police, has been standing back listening to what the police and Richie said to the other, has now decided to have his words heard, "Excuse me officers."

Cargo, who is very upset with Richie says harshly back, "Stand back Mister, this is police business."

Joe will be heard, "What I have to say will also become police business as well."

"Speak."

"This hippie pig, stole records from my record store then he damaged them by throwing them as hard as he could on the sidewalk right in front of me. He threw them so close to me I stepped on them... No I slipped on them and fell down and hurt my... My back."

"Well why didn't you say so?" Cargo says as he walks over to Joe and puts his arm around his shoulders and gives him a gentle shake.

"Joe. I'm Joe."

"Very good Joe, we are very happy that you reported this serious crime to us. Now I want you to look at this guilty hippie pig and tell me for sure if he's the one that stole and damaged your property?"

Joe struts with Cargo's arm around him towards Richie, he looks him straight in his eyes and smiles, "Yup, this is the hippie pig alright."

Richie blurts out nervously, "Betty was suppose to pay for your records man."

Cargo snaps, "Shut up hippie pig and his name is Joe not man. You got that?"

Richie says nothing back. "Well answer me," Cargo demands. "What you lost control of your only weapon, which is that big, hippie pig mouth of yours?"

Richie looks back and forth between three people that look back at him like he has no worth and says nothing. As this is happening and before this, Betty has made her way to her car and is now driving it so she can stop it beside Richie to offer him a chance at a great escape.

Richie, who like the two police men and Joe are totally oblivious to this, almost jumps out of his skin when Betty honks her horn. "Come on Richie, get in, let's get out of here man," Betty yells out to him very nervously, with her head hanging out of her window.

The two police men and Joe who also jumped out of fright look at Betty, like they cannot believe their eyes. Richie acts without thinking, which is very good for him because if he would have thought about it he would have lost his chance at making his escape, for Richie is a slow thinker. On time or with fate's guidance, Richie starts running towards Betty, without saying a word.

"Run Richie, out run those mean pigs," Betty yells in excitement as she slides back into her car and puts it into drive, while her foot is holding down the brake as hard as she can make it.

This all happens in nine seconds. Richie runs, the police men try to grab a hold of him then Joe tries, all attempts fail as Richie keeps on running towards freedom. As he makes it to Betty's car and is opening up the passenger side's door, Bentley pulls out his pistol and points it at him. One second is all it will take for this story to be able to continue on with a chase or a senseless death. Bentley pulls on his trigger then stops as a little old lady walks in front of him with her hat wearing head and stops right in his firing position and says, "Has anyone seen my little dog? My little Buttons?"

8

As Richie gets inside the car panting, Betty takes her heavy foot off the brake and presses it down even heavier on the gas. Skid marks left, the cops run after them with their guns out ready to shoot as the little old lady says to them, "What? Are you going to shoot those people dead for broken records?"

The two police officers look over at the old lady as Joe asks her, "Whose side are you on lady?"

This little old lady that's full of life says, "I'm on the side of life. How about you?"

Joe not impressed says, "You're a confused old broad aren't you?"

"I may be old but at least I'm not a pain in the behind like you are. Do you kiss your mother with that dirty mouth?"

"Go fly off you old Witch."

"Well sonny if you want me to do that then you will have to pull my broom out of your behind."

"Who do you think you're talking to old lady?"

"Why? Don't you know?"

About this time the two confused and having a bad day police officers walk up and Cargo does all the talking again. "That is enough. Joe you step back away from this old lady, we have questions for her."

"Do not call me old lady officers. You will show me some respect for I'm not a criminal. I'm a grandmother, for goodness sake. What is wrong with you men? Are you that full of hate that you can't enjoy life?"

Cargo interrupts, "Look lady, you're in big trouble. You hindered us while we were trying to make an arrest."

9

"Well why are you standing here arguing with me instead of running after them?"

The two police officers look at the other and shake their heads in disgust and start walking away. Joe quickly asks, "What about my records officers?"

Cargo waves his hand in the air while still walking away and asks, "What about them?"

The nameless little old woman looks at Joe and gives him a little laugh and then says, "Sonny, it looks like those hippies got the best of you?"

Joe walks away and says, "To Hell with them old woman."

Still racing down the road Betty and Richie have not said a word to each other besides hello. Richie keeps looking around from front to back, from left to right, trying his best to mellow himself. In his mind he can't take this anymore, something is screaming at him to get out, "Pull over Betty."

"What? Why?"

"I want out."

"We're running away from the police Richie, I don't think it's a good idea to pull over and give them a chance to catch up with us."

"I know but I'm going to get sick. Please pull over the car."

"Alright Richie, we better not get busted."

"We won't Betty, I promise."

Betty pulls over and Richie jumps out of the car and starts running away without closing the door. He gets ten feet away and yells back to Betty, "I'm sorry Betty, you're on your own, I can't go to jail, it would kill me."

In shock Betty yells back, "Where are you going Richie? Get back over here."

"No way Betty. Peace, I hope you make it out of this."

"You ungrateful... Richie get back over here now."

Betty watches as Richie turns a corner and becomes out of sight, 'I can't believe this? How could he leave me alone like this with the police after us? After us? No after me now. Thanks a lot Richie, I hope you trip and land with your face in the mud.'

Betty gets ready to put her car in gear and it shuts off by itself, leaving her with her mouth wide open, 'Now what?' she asks herself.

Betty tries to start her car and it won't crank up, it sounds dead to the world, 'This is just great. Richie this is all your fault. What a day, what's next?'

As Betty asks herself this she suddenly smells apple pie out of nowhere. She looks around then behind her and when she turns back around to look straight in front of herself, she gets quite a surprise, 'Where did this diner come from?'

Betty gets out of her car and reads the sign, 'Eternity's Diner? What kind of name is that? Man this is spaced out, like really far out there.' Betty thinks what should she do as the scent of apple pie comes to her stronger making her stomach rumble, 'Great now I'm hungry, I could stand some french fries and a strawberry shake,'

Betty walks toward Eternity's Diner, she stops and looks back at her car and has a strange feeling flow through her like she will never see it again, 'This is so weird, I'm freaking out. I'm also talking to myself. Well that's not so unusual.' Betty laughs out a little nervous laugh and starts walking towards her unknown, fantastic destiny.

Betty walks into the door of Eternity's Diner and hears music playing she has never heard before. She looks around at the inside of the empty diner and swears she hears voices and the light sound of people eating and drinking. She turns her back to the counter, 'Must be the bunk I smoked," Betty says to herself suspiciously. A heartbeat later she is snapped into reality by a female's voice coming from behind her.

Betty swallows deeply and turns around. "Welcome to Eternity's Diner my child, please have a seat here at the bar," the still pretty looking older lady behind the bar happily says to her, with a trusting smile to boot.

Betty calms herself and breaths out deeply, "Thank you, I think I will have a seat. Can I have a menu please?"

"No need darling, we don't have any menus, for we have only four items that we offer. Fresh baked apple pie of course. We also have coffee, milk and water. Sometimes around the holidays, I'll breakdown and make some of my famous apple cider. What will you have my dear?"

"Who makes the cider?" Another female's voice says out from behind a pair of doors that are directly behind the lady at the bar, which makes Betty stop walking.

"Alright, you can't give me even one can you?" The lady behind the bar yells back to the voice behind the door.

Betty has to know, "Who is that?"

"That is someone you might or might not meet."

Betty who is weirded out, smiles to the nice older lady and says, "I'll take a slice of apple pie and a glass of milk please."

"Coming right up. The jukebox is free, why don't you play a song that you would like to hear, while I get your pie and milk for you. Would you like your pie hot or cold?"

"Hot sounds great, thank you."

Betty turns around and walks over to the strange looking jukebox. This jukebox is lit up brighter than Time's Square. Betty looks deeply at this jukebox watching a display of lighted words read that this song became popular, a hit single in 1983.

"What is this? How can this be? This jukebox says this song is from 1983!"

"Calm down my dear, everything is fine, just the way it is meant to be," the lady behind the bar tells Betty.

"What is meant to be? I don't understand."

"How could you dear, this is your beginning, this is the beginning of everything that will happen. Of everything that will come to be."

"My beginning? You are talking crazy. You must have given me something that makes this whole scene seem like a bad dream or a bad trip?"

"How could I have my dear? You have not eaten or drank anything yet."

"Well maybe it's in the air? Yes that's it, just like the bunk I smoked earlier had a bad smell, so does this diner."

"Eternity's Diner does not stink young lady. It smells of apple pie and love."

"Love? Are you crazy? I smell apple pie but I do not smell love. No what I smell is something really weird, deceitful and space out trippy. That is what I smell? I don't know your name."

"Come over here and read what my tag says my name is, Betty my dear."

"How did you know what my name is?"

"It's on your tag, my dear."

"What? I don't have a tag," Betty looks down at her chest and sees a name tag with her name on it. "Where the Hell did this thing come from?"

"Walk to me my child, and meet your future."

Betty is shaking from a fear that makes her feel like her soul is being pulled in half. Betty holds her breath and looks around Eternity's Diner. Run, run away and out of here is what Betty is telling herself but she has become the deer in the headlights and cannot move an inch nor can she stop holding her breath.

Betty cannot understand why she cannot start breathing again. She tries to scream, nothing comes forth. Betty feels like she is just about to die when she remembers something. Betty to herself. 'She said love, she said love is in the air. All I have to do is believe this, maybe I can save myself?'

Betty gathers herself up with strength she didn't know she obtained inside herself and yells out loud. "I believe in love. I believe inside this diner is the scent of sweet love. Please Universe give me the strength to survive."

Confident and breathing Betty walks over to the older lady behind the bar. She is three steps away as she stops walking and looks the older lady straight into her eyes and feels peace and love inside them. She then looks down at the older lady's name tag, it is the same name tag that lies upon her chest just a little faded from time that has passed by. After Betty blinks she reads the name on the name tag, it reads simply Betty.

14

Betty smiles at her future self and says "Hello."

"Hello younger and prettier self. I have waited for you for fifty years. It's so nice to finally see this happening from the other side of it. Welcome to 2018."

"Well it was a fast trip, I'm hardly even tired," Betty says to her future self.

"That's funny, I forgot I said that."

"I'm not trying to be rude but Betty you look great for seventy years old. You don't even look close to seventy."

"Thanks darling, all though sometimes I feel older than that. Time is time, it never stops or slows down, nor does it speed forward. Saying and knowing this, this diner, this wonderful Eternity's Diner time goes by as stated but within this diner is pockets of time folded over that allows myself to age at a slower pace. I was twenty when you, I walked into this diner, I'm around forty-five now."

"What is going to happen now, um, Betty #1?"

"I don't know Betty #2. In a few minutes I will disappear. I remember from your perspective, I was eating my slice of apple pie that my future self baked from scratch. In between bites I talked to my future self, then she and everybody was gone, I was left all alone with no way of knowing what I was suppose to do next."

"I'm scared Betty."

"Fearing the unknown will not help you in your journey. Look at me and believe that in your future lies a lifetime of pleasantness and good fortune."

"Yes you're right, you look fine and healthy. Can you tell me at least one thing? Are you happy?"

"Yes Betty I'm happy. I lived a great life. This is all I will tell you, for this was all I was told when I asked myself the very same question. That be that, you ready for your pie?"

"Yes Betty, I am."

The young Betty is enjoying her apple pie as her older self disappears right in front of her eyes. Betty is alone as the lights go out inside Eternity's Diner. Betty hears a low hum in the darkness as a push forward through time comes to Eternity's Diner. Betty is stunned and nervous. She thinks about getting out of her seat when everything stops and becomes calm. Betty looks around in the darkness as the bright lights come back on revealing her older self standing in the same spot she just disappeared from a moment ago.

Two Betty's stare at the other, one smiling, the other still nervous. Betty one breaks the silence, "Fooled you, Me."

"What's going on? You freaked me out."

"Yes I know, this happened to me when I was you."

"Yeah right... But you still could have warned me."

"What's the fun in that younger me?"

"Fun? Older me, I am not having fun."

"Don't worry younger me, you will and lots of it."

"How?"

"Men."

"Men?"

"Yes men. You, I, we have lots and lots of free having, hot sex with a lot of men. All of them strangers."

"You are tripping out older me if you think I'm going to let a lot of men have their way with me."

"It's not them having their way with us, no my dear, it's us having our way with them."

"No way, I don't think so. This can't be true? Can it?"

Betty one stares at Betty two and can't hold back her laughter any longer. Betty two watches her older self laugh her heart out for about fifteen seconds until she starts laughing as well. "I see I still have my wicked sense of humor as I grow older."

"It becomes even more wicked as time and years fly by."

"So older me, what is really going on? Am I really a floozy, or are you messing with me?"

"All the way to the top, younger me."

"I don't understand?"

"Yes I'm messing with you. I thought lightening the mood would help you relax."

"Is that true?"

"Yes and no. I'm only doing what I did years ago when I was you."

"I think I understand."

"Good, because I did when I was you, well almost."

"Now what Betty one?"

"We become one."

"Aren't we already?"

"Again, yes and no."

"Please Betty one, you're starting to drive me crazy."

"Nope it's the bunk you smoked that's doing that to you."

Both Betty's have a good laugh, "I guess you remember about the grass and Richie."

"Yes what a butt head for running away like that. After I entered Eternity's Diner he came back and drove off with my car."

"No way?"

"Want to see it happening for yourself?"

"I guess you know that answer."

"He won't be able to see Eternity's Diner so he will not be able to see us as well." Betty one leads Betty two to the door so she can look out it. What she sees is Richie looking around her car and not calling out for her. He shrugs his shoulders and gets behind the wheel and starts up her car without trouble, "Don't that just tick you off? You can't start your car up but he can?"

"Yes that ticks me off alright but what the heck it's not like I'm going to be needing it. Am I?"

"Not in this life time."

"I like my car."

"I know, for so did I. You ready to merge together."

"Is it going to hurt?"

"I don't remember."

"Is that a joke?"

"Yes and a very bad one at that. Pain is part of life. This is the second time we have done this. The first time I was you and you now are the second time as well."

"How does this all work?"

"Time and space are very temperamental entities."

"Meaning?"

"When I was you there was no myself as I am now."

"What?"

"I did my part to start all of this, I entered Eternity's Diner. Who I encountered was an older version of myself from the future. Since I started this, I had no older version of myself to encounter so my version of my older self came from a future that has not happened yet."

"Again I say what?"

"You Betty, you are the final element to make all this time and space become the normal path for your life."

"How can I do this?"

"By living the same life I lived up until now."

"I still don't understand?"

"Betty as soon as you become me, the me I am today, you will in fact become the older Betty I encountered fifty years ago in this very same Eternity's Diner. Understand now?"

"I think so?" Betty stands up taller, "Yes I understand, I am I, I am you and together we will become the only Betty."

"You got it my dear."

"How do we become one?"

"Apple pie... As soon as we share an apple pie together, I will not be here anymore. The apple pies you smell will not be here, everything will be started back from the beginning. You will have to learn how to make apple pies."

"I will? I thought someone else will be doing this? You know, the voice behind those doors?"

"Well that's up to you Betty. This all comes down to a single choice you have to make. Do you let things be or do you change things?"

"Change what things?"

"That's for you to find out for yourself."

"I don't like this. What if I screw it all up? What if I make the wrong choice?"

"Then Betty, we will never meet."

"That's all? Well no big deal then. I'll be able to manage this without any trouble getting in my way."

"I'm sure of it as well."

"I was being sarcastic Betty."

"Yes I know Betty."

"I guess you do. We could go around and around like this all day, couldn't we older me?"

"Yes we could but we have more important things to do right now younger me."

"Yes we do... I have to know one thing?"

"What's that?"

"Who's driving this Eternity's Diner? I mean who's in control of it?"

"You are Betty."

"Don't give me that Betty. Who is the one that makes Eternity's Diner go back and forth through time?"

Older Betty smiles like she knows the biggest secret in the world and enjoys the fact that she not telling it, "That in time will become known to you."

"That sounds eerie?"

"And could become that... If you make the wrong choice."

"Tell me Betty?"

"Nope Younger me. There are just some things you have to learn for yourself, all by yourself."

"Thanks for nothing."

"Getting mad at me will not change things. I made mistakes, I made wrong choices. Which if you do not make this time will be erased, just like I never made them."

"Then for goodness sake, tell me the mistakes you made so I won't repeat them this time around."

"Nope, things don't work like that. You have to live your life just like I did mine. Remember this, you have an advantage that I did not."

"I do? What is this advantage?"

"Me."

"Huh?"

"When we merge, I will be part of you."

"You will be my guide to make sure I make the right decisions and not the wrong ones?"

"Nope."

"Then what?"

"I'll become the voice in the back of your mind that almost silently gives you encouragement."

"But all final decisions are mine to make?"

"Correct."

"Well let's get this over with."

"That's the spirit. Let's share some pie, shall we?"

"Let's."

The ceremony of the eating of the apple pie between the two Betty's is just that. It's more of a first and a last goodbye that is about to happen between them. Apple pie is finished between two friends that are the same person in fact. The older Betty knows what is about to happen so she takes a hold of the her younger version's hand and says, "Goodbye Betty, see you in the funny pages."

"Goodbye," Betty says to an empty Eternity's Diner. She lets out a deep breath then she's scared stiff from a loud buzzing sound that comes from an intercom that just appeared on the counter. She doesn't know what to do so she leans forward to look at it and it buzzes again, scaring her in return.

A male's voice comes from the intercom, "You there?"

Betty quietly answers back, "Yes I am."

"Good... It is time we take our first time travel together."

"Okay, I guess? Who are you?"

"I'm Eternity's Diner, Betty."

"What does that mean?"

"I'm the voice over the intercom that tells you when it's time that we time travel."

"So you are just a voice and not a person?"

"I'm the voice of the being that is Eternity's Diner."

"Can you make this more clear please?"

"Maybe later, we have work to do. We have to meet Mary Brown so she can teach you how to make her very special, her one of a kind apple pies."

"Let's meet her then, I'm starting to get hungry and lonely,"

"Very good Betty. Now hold on tight, the first time one experiences time travel, it can be a little unsettling."

"I can imagine," Betty adds.

Betty closes her eyes and Eternity's Diner travels into the future of only five years from Betty's 1969.

The second person that is allowed to enter Eternity's Diner is a nice old lady from New Jersey. The year is 1973, the month is November and the day is the tenth. Mary Brown, who is sixty four walks down the same sidewalks she has done the past thirty four years.

Mary moved to this neighborhood when she was thirty, the same year she and her husband, Eric were married. Together they lived the past thirty two years here. Mary has lived an additional two years alone, after his death. The neighborhood has changed many times over, still Mary remembers these changes and is glad to share her stories with whomever has the time to stop and talk to her.

Mary to herself, "It is so cold, my hands are numb. It would be so nice if a boy from the neighborhood would carry my groceries home for me. Times ago nice boys would do that for old ladies like myself. Where have the good days gone to? I fear the years ahead, I guess I'm lucky I don't have that many to live. Stop that crazy talk Mary, you have to get home and bake a fresh apple pie for Eric's memory because he loved them so much."

Mary stops walking, stopping for a moment because the pain in her legs and feet has became stronger. Two minutes later Mary is walking on and still talking to herself.

"Eric, I loved that silly and loving man. He always told me after he ate a slice or two of my fresh baked apple pie, that he would marry me all over again just so he could eat my apple pies. What is this place? This diner was not here before, I know it. I would have stopped in for a cup of tea and a chance to take a rest for awhile. Eternity's Diner, that is a strange name for a diner. Oh well, I don't care about names all I care about is if the place is nice and warm and so is the tea. It's funny I don't smell any food being cooked coming from this Eternity's Diner. I wonder what that is about?"

Mary slowly opens the door of Eternity's Diner and walks through it to be greeted by a smiling Betty. Betty says to Mary, "Hello Mary it's so nice to meet you, please come in and have a seat."

Mary looks around inside the empty diner and asks, "Did you just open up? Wait... How do you know my name is

Mary? Who are you? What is this place?"

"Mary I am Betty. This place is Eternity's Diner, it is a very special place. This place is so special that it stays only in one spot for a little while."

Mary looks confused and worried. "What are you talking about young lady? How can a diner move one place to another, is it magic or something? What is your name again, my dear?"

"My name is Betty. Yes this diner can move from one place to another. And not only that it can move through time. On how I knew your name and that you were coming is because Eternity's Diner told me so."

"Betty is it? Well Betty in my time we had a saying for people that talked like you do and that is you're crazy out of your mind," Mary says with a little laugh at the end.

"Mary you are funny, sweet old lady."

"Who you calling a old lady, young lady? Didn't your mother teach you better than that?"

"Yes ma'am, Mary. I'm sorry. Let's start over shall we? I am Betty, I'm the caretaker of Eternity's Diner. I need you Mary, I need your help."

"What kinda of help could you possibly need from me Betty, I'm just a tired old lady?"

"Apple pie. I need you to teach me how to bake your famous apple pies for my future customers."

"My apple pie? Why would you need me to teach you how to bake an apple pie? This is a diner don't you already have apple pie on the menu? If you don't shame on you."

"We, I, Eternity's Diner doesn't have anything on a menu,

we don't even have a menu and apparently we never will."

"Look Betty, I do not know what kind of silly talk you are trying to get me to understand? But I will have none of it, you hear me young lady?"

"Yes ma'am. But I promise you this, that what I'm saying to you is the truth and not silly talk."

"Why my pies Betty? What's so special about them?"

"Eternity's Diner tells me it is the best apple pie recipe of all time. Eternity's Diner wants to be able to give its future customers the best tasting apple pie they have ever had."

"That makes sense. What am I talking about? Now you got me talking silly about a diner telling you to have me teach you how to bake my fresh apple pies."

"Think about this Mary, what do you have to lose? Your apple pie will be the only pie ever served here at Eternity's Diner. To be honest with you Mary, your apple pie will be the only kind of food ever served here."

"That is even more silly. How can a diner only serve apple pie? What no soup? No fried chicken? No hamburgers? Young lady, I think you are trying to make a fool out of me."

"No Mary, I swear to you I am not trying to make a fool out of you."

"Maybe so but I have no more time for this, I'm leaving."

Betty looks over at the intercom. She waits but no voice comes out from it so she asks, "Well Eternity's Diner, I tried my best but Mary won't help me?"

"Try crying, that helps sometimes."

Betty looks at Mary and it seems like she didn't hear the

voice of Eternity's Diner, "Yes it is true that Mary cannot hear me." Betty shrugs and takes a seat in one of the many empty booths so she can put her head down and cry.

"My dear, let's have none of this. Okay Betty, I don't understand but if teaching you how to make one of my apple pies is all you need from me, well it's the least I can do for you. You seem like a nice young lady, a very confused one but nice and I like to help nice people out when I can."

"Thank you Mary, thank you very much."

"Don't think anything about it my dear. Now dry your eyes and take me to your kitchen so we can get started."

"Betty, everything you will need to bake an apple pie is inside Mary's groceries bag." Eternity's Diner informs.

"Sounds great Mary, please follow me, here let me carry your bag of groceries. Eternity's Diner has told me that everything we will need is inside these bag of groceries."

"Yes my dear that is true. I was going to bake one when I got home later tonight."

In the kitchen Betty is taking out the groceries from the bags. Every item she needs to make an apple pie when placed on the tabletop that item is duplicated in mass quantities inside the cabinets. Mary looked around the kitchen when she first entered and noticed that all the cabinets were empty. When they started to become filled up Mary had no idea how this happened and thought it was better no to ask Betty how it happened.

"Look at this Mary, every cabinet stocked full for my customers, perhaps for eternity."

"Yes dear. This is very weird. Oh well, let's get to baking."

"Betty tell Mary this.... Then after you bake your apple pies tell her this..."

"Thank you Mary, after we're through, I and Eternity's Diner have a present for you."

"Really? What kind of present? Is it money?"

"Much better than money Mary. Please wait for the baking of your wonderful apple pies and they are cooling before I enlighten you on your present that is more like a gift. I'll tell you one thing Mary, this gift you cannot hold in your hands but you can feel it, see it, smell it, hear it. How's that for weird Mary?"

"Very much so Betty. I just don't know about the youth of today? Where are your minds at? All these changes that you yell for with so many angry voices? What you all need is more apple pie and less, what do you call it? Oh yeah pot, or is it weed? Or is it grass, Betty?"

"It's all the above Mary. And good for you for being aware of things we youth want and need. There are worst things on this planet than getting high."

"That's very true young lady but shame on you for being one of those hippie people that like to get high and have sex. In my day, we waited 'til we got married before any hanky-panky went on."

"Oh yes everyone was so good and proper before. My generation ruined the whole world. If it were so easy Mary. The world has been on a downward spiral until this day. My generation just wants to live free for the day. No more wars, no more unnecessary deaths, just lots of love."

"Love thy neighbor Betty, this is true, however always keep both eyes open on neighbor's that look at you like you are in their way. Respect thy elders and our history."

"Yes Mary, I do. Now where do we start?"

"Well Betty first things first. You watch me, you watch what I do, while making your very own apple pie with only your hands, for mine will not touch it even once."

"Why Mary? I need to be able to bake the best apple pies for Eternity's Diner."

"And you will Betty. Trust me my dear, you will make me proud. You know how I know this Betty? I'll tell you why. It is because I'm going to make you bake pie after pie 'til one is perfect. It's up to you on how many pies I make you bake. Watch me closely, learn quickly. Talk and not pay attention, learn slowly."

"Wow Mary, you sound so stern."

"Damn right, young lady. My apple pies made my husband love me even more. My apple pie was the last thing he tasted before he died. You see Betty my husband Eric was dying in a hospital. All Eric wanted from me before he slipped away to death was a final kiss from me and one last bite of one of my world famous apple pies."

"Wow dig it, what a heavy and loving tale you have to tell Mary. The hairs on my arms are standing up. Mary I promise I will do your world famous apple pies justice."

"Thank you Betty, that makes me feel good."

"Alright Mary you lead and I will mimic your every move."

"Hang on Betty, there is one more thing I want to tell you. For some reason I don't know why," Mary pauses. "I feel deep inside my soul, if I don't tell you my secret, I will never be able to tell my secret to anyone."

"Always go with your feelings Mary. They are your conscious trying to inform you to do the right thing."

"Very wise my dear. I can't believe I'm telling anyone this. Eric was not allowed food other than what was on his menu. My apple pie was not on his menu so I sneaked in a piece for him. I leaned over my love, my husband, looked him in his eyes told him I loved him, I gave him a kiss, then I placed a small piece of my apple pie inside his mouth. Then..."

Mary's body starts to shake from unseen pain as her eyes tear up so her crying can have a prelude to its swan song. Mary walks over to Betty's open arms and places her head down upon Betty's chest for comfort and love. Mary cries hard then harder until the weight of her secret causes her to collapse to the floor, sending a trying to stop her from falling to the floor Betty with her.

Mary still crying tries to talk, "Oh Betty, I can't believe what I did. I am so terrible, Betty I did so bad. My husband, I killed my husband."

"What? How? Why Mary?"

"Betty after I put that small piece of apple pie in Eric's mouth he chewed it for about three seconds and then he started to choke and he couldn't stop. Betty I made my husband choke to death on my apple pie. Lord bless my soul, how could I do that to Eric? How could I be so stupid? How could I be so uncaring? How could I..."

"Mary stop it. You did not kill Eric. You with love in your heart and soul for Eric, Mary you helped him let go of life so his soul could pass on leaving his body safe from not being in any pain anymore."

Mary stops crying and starts laughing leaving a puzzled Betty staring at her like what's her problem.

"Betty my dear, you should put that on a greeting card. I killed my husband and you make me look and feel like a saint. I don't know if I'm happy or sad? But I feel in my heart you meant from your heart what you said to be true. You think I helped out Eric on his journey to the afterlife just like that. And I, for years have carried this burden on my soul, like a heavy weight that I could barely lift. Maybe there is something to your generation and all this freedom you talk about."

"Peace and love is a beautiful thing Mary. I don't know if this helps or not Mary but I forgive you for Eric's death."

"Thank you my dear, it helps a little. Still this weight feels heavy Betty but it does feel good to finally get all of this out. Thank you for listening to an old woman's dark secret. You are a good person Betty."

"And so are you Mary. Now let's make some history shall we Mary?"

"Yes my dear, let's show your future guests what my apple pies are all about."

Mary shows Betty how to create the perfect apple pie. Mary smiles after tasting Betty's apple pie for it tastes just like she baked it herself. Still out of sternness and wanting to know if Betty could do the same without her help she has Betty make and bake another one just to be sure.

A little later, "Well Betty my dear, this pie is perfect, you should be very proud of yourself, I couldn't do any better."

"Thank you Mary, I know I baked it but wow, it was your recipe that made the whole difference. I have to say Mary, this is the best tasting apple pie I've ever tasted."

"I know my dear and now you know my secret. Both of them. My poor Eric's death and how I use half apples and half pears to make my pies so different and so delicious."

"Your secrets are safe with me, I promise. Thank you Mary you have helped me and Eternity's Diner.

For your great deed are you ready for your gift?"

"Yes Betty my dear, Give me something special."

"Mary, Eternity's Diner has the power to take you back in time to a day that you would like to return to."

"That is so wonderful Betty. Take me back to the day that Eric and I got married, so I can tell him I love him still to this day with all my heart."

"No Mary it doesn't work that way. You can go back to the day you were married but cannot interact with yourself or Eric. Sorry Mary those are the rules."

"Some rules Betty. What is the reason to go back in time if I cannot do what I want to do?"

"Think of it as a last request Mary."

"What do you mean Betty? Are you saying what I'm thinking that your saying, that I'm dying?"

"Yes Mary, I'm sorry, tomorrow is the day you are suppose to die."

"What from Betty? How do I die?"

"Heart attack, you die from a heart attack Mary."

"Well Betty, all I have to say is, that this is a big bummer."

"I know Mary but you, your memory will live on through your apple pies."

"Well at least there is that I guess Betty."

"Time is coming Mary. Do you want to leave Eternity's Diner this day at this time on Earth or do you want to go back to a past that you hold dear and die there?"

"Take me back Betty, take me back in time. I would like that very much. Can I go to Eric just to see him?"

"Yes Mary that would be fine. Eric, if he sees you, would not know who you are. For you will go to the past the same age you are now."

"So I guess I could actually talk to Eric and myself for a fact as long as I do not tell them who I am. Is that right Betty?"

"Yes Mary, that is right. But if I were you, I would not do that. The temptation to tell them who you are and the fact that you might want to give them warnings about the future would win out. And that Mary would be a very bad thing to do. If you change anything Mary, you will never have this gift given to you."

"I understand Betty, my sweet dear. I will hear Eric's voice if I get the chance and maybe mine as well. But I will not give any warnings of the future, this I promise to you and Eternity's Diner."

"Very well Mary. Hold on tight, we will set you down as close to the church you got married in as we can. Enjoy yourself Mary, thank you and goodbye."

"Goodbye my dear, give me a hug."

Mary steps out of Eternity's Diner on the day she and Eric got married. She watches as the happy couple they were walk out of the church so much in love. The next day as the sun is rising in the morning sky, Mary died alone sitting on a park bench.

...There is a darker version of Eternity's Diner included in and titled for the first edition of Dark Stories for the Mind. What has happened so far in chapter one of this version (Betty's Eternity's Diner) is a mixture of original and new content. What comes next is a new lighter and a lot less darker version. I was going to start this lighter version right before the forbidden kiss Betty receives in the original darker version. To keep this second version lighter I eliminated the possibility of the temptation of the forbidden kiss Betty either agreed to or say nay to. I am where you are at right now as I write this to you... I have no idea what is going to happen to Betty, however I am determined to have a great time finding out.

Keith Starblue

Chapter Two:

Betty is standing and looking out the door's to Eternity's Diner. Tears flow from her eyes in heavy streams as she stares at the dead body of Mary, "It's not fair... Why did Mary have to die?"

"It was her time. Feel happy for her, she died happy. If she was left alone, if not for us, she would have died all alone without the chance to share her gift with us."

Betty snaps around very upset, "That's what this is all about isn't?"

"What are you asking me Betty?"

"It wasn't about Mary, is was about what she could do for you... For us?"

"If you want to be negative and think of it that way then yes, we are users instead of helpers."

"I don't think I like this anymore."

34

"Do you want out?"

"Maybe... I don't know?"

"It would be better sooner than later if you left us."

"What us? You're a voice on an intercom."

"I am much more than that Betty."

"Yes I know, you have the ability to time travel."

"Yes and no."

"What are you saying?"

"We have the ability, together to time travel."

"Without me?"

"This would all end. The years ahead, the three of us will share together..."

"Three of us?"

"Yes, you do remember the lady's voice coming from behind the doors, when you met your older self?"

"Yes I do."

"Good. The three of us helping people and receiving back from them. You will be giving up these fifty years."

"Yes but are these future fifty years truly mine? What of the life I was to live these fifty years outside the doors of this Eternity's Diner?"

"In a way you are."

"Do not confuse me Eternity's Diner, say what you mean."

"Very well. The older you that you just met?"

"Yes?"

"She is living the life, you would have lived."

"How is this possible?"

"She is you Betty."

"I don't understand?"

"She came into Eternity's Diner, she stayed and lived fifty years with us. Even though all this became possible from the future you are getting ready to live, it is a fact it happened. The older you, was only half of the equation, you are the second, the last part. If you do not live these years, the older you, you met will never come to be."

"My mind's on fire. You're tripping me out."

"Sorry... The beginning and the end... You and your older self have to meet like you just did this year of 1969 and fifty years from now in the year 2018."

"I'm trying to understand."

"I know you are Betty... It's a circle, your older self has went her half way. She lived her fifty years, it is time that you did the same thing. This way you can become her and meet your younger self for the first time. If you complete the circle, the circle can continue for infinity."

"Really?"

"I like to think so."

"But you don't know for sure, do you?"

"No, for it has not happened. I'm not really sure what's

going to happen when you the final Betty meets your younger self for the first time."

"What do you mean?"

"For all I know, when this happens, everything might close up on itself like it never happened at all."

"I don't like this."

"It's a mystery I want to live and know Betty. I gave myself, my life to become Eternity's Diner. I've enjoyed the last fifty years I've been Eternity's Diner. I want to re-live them again."

"Why?"

"I, you, we made mistakes. Not big ones, for this is not what this is all about."

"We made small mistakes."

"Yes and we made small helps. A lot more small helps than we made mistakes, I'm happy to say."

"Well that's good. Still I don't know. So my first self, which was just my older self is living my life right now?"

"Yes. To her, to you, Richie took off running and she, you, drove away. Your, her, car never stopped running."

"And I have to complete the circle to allow her to live this life. Tell me, is she happy?"

"Yes, she lives a happy life. She gets married, she has children. Later she has grandchildren. She dies with love in her heart for her family that loves her very much."

"Sounds nice."

"It is, she lives a happy and long life."

"What about me?"

"That's up to you. What do you want?"

"I don't know. I don't know what to ask for or even want."

"Mary."

"What about her?"

"Do you want her back alive?"

"Back alive? Like a zombie?"

Eternity's Diner laughs, "Oh Betty, I forgot how funny that was when you said it the first time."

"I'm glad to please you."

"I'm sorry, I forgot to ask you."

"Ask me what?"

"Do you want to get high?"

"High?"

"Very much so."

"That's allowed?"

"Of course Betty. This is your life, you're not in prison here inside Eternity's Diner."

"That's nice to know."

"You have a life Betty. You have fun, you party, you even have sex from time to time."

"I do? I don't know about that."

"What do you not know about it? You are a living human being getting ready to live a life like no other before you has. Live it Betty."

"Alright I will. If I want to find out what happens next, I guess I have to live it to find out?"

"Correct. You want to get high?"

"What, all by myself?"

"Yes."

"What's the fun in that?"

"It didn't stop you the last time."

"So is this all I do is get high all the time?"

"No. First you help someone, then you come back to Eternity's Diner..."

"Then I get high, all by myself."

"Yes and no."

"Do not start that."

"I'll eventually be able to get high with you."

"You will? How?"

"Time will only tell Betty."

"But first comes Mary?"

"Yes. Do you really want to spend the next fifty years baking apple pies?"

"No, not really."

"Good, then let's go pick up Mary so she can do this for you, for us."

"She'll agree?"

"Wouldn't you?"

"I don't know?"

"You will walk up to her right before she dies and ask her if she wants to live on with us instead of dying alone."

"That's so cold."

"It is? Why?"

"We're asking her to give up her..."

"Her what? Her death?"

"I guess you're right?"

"You'll never know unless you ask her."

"I'm having a feeling."

"Tell me about this feeling?"

"Asking."

"What about it?"

"That's what I do, isn't it? I ask people if they want my, our help before they die?"

"Yes. You are their last chance. Perhaps the one thing they like to say or finish before their deaths."

"No wonder I get high all the time. It sounds so, it seems so depressing?"

"Only if you think of it that way."

"You're a big help."

"I am."

"I was being sarcastic."

"I know. You help a lot of people out."

"How many?"

"About one a day."

"For the next fifty years?"

"Yes."

"That's a lot of people."

"You can handle it, you can handle them."

"Can I?"

"You did the last time."

"Yes but I also made mistakes?"

"Yes."

"Mistakes I can correct?"

"Yes."

"What the Hell, it's like I'm living two lives. If I fail this one than my other life, a one that I will never know, will continue on. She will have a good life if I live my life here inside Eternity's Diner. This circle will allow myself to leave my mark on Earth."

"Beautifully said Betty."

"Thank you... What is your name?"

"Later."

"No, now."

"I can't, it will ruin everything, the big surprise."

"I can't deal with that."

"What do you mean Betty."

"I'm walking, I'm leaving, if I do not get what I want."

"What is this want, you want Betty?"

"Control."

"Control over what?"

"My life, my fate, my world, my rules."

"You dare?"

"Better believe it Eternity's Diner. I've been listening to you and I do not like it."

"What is there for you not to like Betty?"

"You tell me what and when. We appear, I go out and have an adventure, while you what? Wait for me to come back so you can tell me what to do after that and so on."

"It's the design of it all."

"What a crock... You throw the stick, I go fetch it for you."

"It's not like that Betty..."

"I don't want to hear it, I'm out."

"Power, I can give you power."

"And there it is, the darkness that's out of sight from human eyes. Your forked tongue will not sway I."

"What are you talking about Betty? This is not like you."

"I'm not the Betty you know Eternity's Diner. I'm me, I'm my own Betty. You said I have love affairs?"

"Yes I did."

"Well then I feel I'm the one that gets to choose who my love affairs are with."

"That's not the way it happened last time."

"So what? You point at some random man and I go over to him and take off my clothes?"

"It's not like that Betty. You leave to help someone, that's what I find for you. What you do after you get there is all up to you, I have no say in it."

"That's a little bit better, still I don't know? I think I'd be better off if I leave now and save myself some unknown trouble later."

"Betty I can't believe this? This is not you."

"What can I say? I guess I'll repeat myself. I'm my own kind of Betty."

"I see... What can I say but welcome Betty as you are.

Eternity's Diner is yours to do with as you please."

"Can Eternity's Diner cause harm?" No response. Betty waits seven seconds, "Answer me. Can Eternity's..."

"Yes it can."

"That's good to know. Show me some harm that you can cause for me."

"No I cannot."

"Do it or I will leave."

"Please Betty, I cannot, I will not. I love you Betty, please become who you were before."

"No way man, what a drag. I feel like being the bad guy? What am I saying? I want to be the bad lady."

"No I will not allow this to become true."

"What are you going to do about it? You're a voice, nothing more. You do not have it in you to rock my world. No wonder I find excitement elsewhere."

"Betty are you trying to make me mad?"

Betty pauses and looks around, "No way man, I'm just being me."

"I do not think so Betty?"

"Fine... Yes I was trying to make you mad."

"Why?"

"To see what you would do. I wanted to know for sure if I can trust you with my life."

"Did I pass your test?"

"I do not know yet. I'll get back to you later about it."

"Fair enough. Do you want to pick up Mary or do I pick someone else we, you what to meet?"

"Why do I? Why do we need Mary?"

"So she can bake her apple pies. She complains about it but deep inside she's having the time of her life. She just loves to watch people from through out time try her apple pies for the first time."

"What people?"

"Excuse me?"

"What people? I leave here, I go out there, they do not come here."

"All that you help that are to die afterwards come here for a slice of apple pie with conversation before we move on."

"What happens to these apple pie eaters? What happens when we move on?"

"They leave Eternity's Diner and live out the rest of their lives. However long that is."

"We don't, I don't know, capture their souls?"

"What? Why would you ask that?"

"Are you evil Eternity's Diner?"

"Not if you are the same Betty as before. If you are the one that is evil or wants bad things to happen, yes I will become evil as well."

"What a bummer. What's the old saying? I remember now, it sucks to be you."

"What are you saying Betty?"

"I'm leaving."

"Please all this will end."

"You mean you will end. Myself I will go on."

"Yes this it true. I can't exist without you."

"Do you want me to make you become evil?"

"No."

"Will you become evil if I command you to?"

"I would not want to but I would, if it meant being with you for the next fifty years."

"Oh you love me this much Eternity's Diner?"

"Yes I do, I love you with all my heart."

"What heart? You're not a being, you're a simple voice."

"There is nothing simple about myself, Betty."

"Is that bragging I hear?"

"No, it is the truth."

"Please spare me."

"You do not believe me?"

"No, I do not."

"What can I do to prove it to you?"

"Show me your face."

"I can't."

"Why not?"

"I'm not ready to be seen as of yet."

"Why not?"

"I can't tell you, you wouldn't understand."

"Tell me or I'll walk."

"In truth..."

"Yes."

"I don't really exist as of yet."

"What are you?"

"I'm an echo from the future that was sent back to the past to be with you until..."

"Until what?"

"Until we meet for the first time."

"When are you from? What year?"

"2018"

"Fifty years from now?"

"Yes."

"What, do we meet at the last minute right before I'm to

meet myself for the first time again?"

"Not at the last minute..."

"Is it worth the wait? This love of ours?"

"I'd like to think so."

"But you don't know for sure do you? You're not really here, you're just an echo. Can you even feel real love?"

"What I am now feels love for you from the past fifty years we lived together the first time."

"This is so weird. To me it still feels like I'm setting myself up for a great big bummer."

"If you feel that future love is a bummer, I guess that it is."

"I would have to give you lots of trust."

"Yes but you can trust me."

"So you keep saying. I'd like you to know that my mom didn't raise me to be a fool."

"I know this Betty. Trust me I mean you no harm."

"You will not do evil unless I tell you to?"

"I will not."

"Okay I'll trust you Eternity's Diner. But there is one thing you need to know."

"What is that Betty?"

"I will never ask you to do something evil."

"I know Betty, for you are a good person that does good."

"So you trust me?"

"Yes I do Betty."

"You trust me not to ask you to do evil things?"

"Yes I do Betty."

"I can trust you with the next fifty years of my life?"

"Yes you can Betty."

"Then let's go pick up Mary before she dies and get this circle rocking and a rolling."

"Right away Betty."

"Wait, why can't I just walk out the door right now and go get Mary?"

"Because Betty, Mary is dead at this moment."

"I can't bring her in here and you bring her back to life?"

"I do not have that power. I prolong life only, I cannot bring it back to life."

"Then we go back in time just a few minutes ago?"

"Yes, where she'll still be alive."

"Mary will live with us for the next fifty years?"

"She will live within her own pocket of time. I'm going to create a time loop for her so everyday to her will be the same day, the day she was to die."

"What happens if Mary leaves this pocket of time?"

"She will die."

"I guess we better explain this to her more than once, she is really old and I don't want her to forget."

"Mary's age will not be a problem for her. The longer she stays inside Eternity's Diner, the more refreshed her mind, body and spirit will become."

"Are we there yet?"

"I haven't even started our time travel backwards yet."

"Well what are you waiting for? Time jump away."

Eternity's Diner is Back in time. Betty runs to the doors, it is night as a smile lightens up her face. Mary is sitting on the park bench and she is still alive. Betty thinks to herself that she has plenty of time to convince her. For Mary will stay alive until the sun rises.

Betty walks out of the doors to Eternity's Diner wondering what she's going to say to Mary. One thing she knows not to do is to walk up behind Mary and say hello. The problem is Mary is sitting with her back to Betty so Betty walks a wide path before making re-contact with Mary.

As Betty gets closer to Mary, Mary notices her and waves her over. Betty picks up her speed and gets there in half the time she was going to take and sits down beside Mary, "Hello my Dear. Have you come to see me off?"

"No I haven't Mary, I've come to take you back with me to Eternity's Diner."

"Thank you My Dear, but no. I've had enough of that strange place, it gave me the creeps. I am glad to share my apple pies with whomever comes after me but I don't want to be there when they try it."

"Are you sure Mary? I'm offering you fifty years."

"That would make me how old? Forget it I don't want to know. I do not want to live another fifty years only getting older and older."

"You don't have to get older. I mean you won't get older."

"I'll get younger, Betty?" Mary asks happily.

"No afraid not Mary. You will stay the age you are now."

"That's not fair, you get to be young."

"I am young, you are old."

"That was hard young lady and kind of cold."

"I'm sorry Mary, I'm new to this whole helping people out."

"Some help, I get to be old and not pretty like you."

"There's nothing I can do about this Mary."

"Are you sure?"

"I think so?"

"Did you ask Eternity's Diner if this was possible?"

"No."

"Why not My Dear?"

"To be honest Mary, I didn't even think about it."

"And why not?"

"Because saving your life was the only thing on my mind."

"That is the sweetest thing anyone has ever said to me."

"And I mean it Mary... Will you come with me and bake your apple pies for total strangers through out time?"

"I bake? I thought that was your honor?"

"Change of Plans."

"Is that a fact? How do you young folks say it? I think this is the way it goes Betty, What a bummer."

Betty laughs. "Yes laugh at me Betty, that will help."

"I'm laughing with you Mary, don't be so hard."

"Life has made me this way Betty. I'm all alone and I do not want to be."

"Come with me then."

"No way. If I go with you I want to become young. I want my sexy built body back. This time around, I'm going to enjoy it too."

"Mary, that's like really bad."

"Speak for yourself young lady. If you look at me like I am now and add sex to it yes this would be bad. If I was as young as you, I'd put you to shame."

"Is that a fact? I don't think so Mary, look at me."

"Yes Betty you are a Betty but if I was my younger self..."

"Then what Mary?"

"If we were sitting together and a man came up to us he would only talk to you after I told him no."

"Is that so? Mary I like you but you're starting to make me a little mad. Here I go and offer you..."

"Offer me fifty years of being old and baking apple pie after apple pie for strangers for these fifty years?"

Betty looks at Mary and understands and she wonders why it took this long for her to understand Mary's concerns. "You're right Mary, you should be able to be young."

"That is what I'm saying Betty. Just think about it if I'm young I'll never call you My Dear again. Wouldn't you like that My Dear?"

"Yes I would Mary."

"Then let's go inside Eternity's Diner and demand that it makes me become young again. The same age you are would be just fine."

"Yes let's do that. Wait I don't think it can do that for you but I have an idea."

"What is it My... Betty?"

"I found out something Mary. I found out that Eternity's Diner takes orders from me."

"It does?"

"Yes it does so I will command it to go back in time to when you are my age..."

"Yes?"

"Then you as you are now will switch places with your younger self. She will come with me and you will have to stay back in the time before electricity."

"My Dear you are quite the smart ass."

"Thank you old lady, would you like a cup of tea before you take your nap?"

"Why are you being this way to me Betty?"

"Payback Mary for saying what you said about if the two of us was sitting together."

"Bitter pill My Dear. How old are you anyway?"

"I'm twenty."

"What a great age."

"Thank you, I like it."

"I don't know?"

"You don't know what Mary?"

"I do not think you'll be able to handle the competition of I at the age of twenty."

"Don't worry about me, worry about yourself. What you see me like now, is all natural. Just wait until I doll myself up. I can make men's hearts stop beating when they lay eyes upon me, when I look ready for loving."

"Is that so? Well the same goes for me My Dear."

Betty stands up, "Let's make this happen Mary. One thing though I'm afraid."

"What is that?"

"You will still have to be the one to bake all the apple pies. I'll be all hot looking ready for a date with some handsome stranger and you'll be up to your eyebrows in baking powder. Isn't that a gas?"

"No it is not," Mary proclaims as she stands up slowly, "It is no gas at all, it's a bummer. You know Betty you are a bummer. Forget the whole thing."

"Suit yourself Mary."

Mary stares at Betty with ice cold eyes then she smiles and then she adds a little laugh, "Damn, I forgot what the passion feels like for life and love when one is young. Thank you Betty. If I have to bake bunches of apple pies for the next fifty years to get my youth back, it's worth it."

"So you are saying yes Mary?"

"As long as I'm young and fine. One thing."

"What's that?"

"Some times I will be the one to go out on a date with a handsome stranger while you bake the pies. I get three days a week, you get four."

"No way Mary, this tale that is to be told is mine. I get five days, you get two days."

"Alright as long as one of my days is either a Friday or Saturday night."

"That's fair."

"No Betty fair would be four and three."

"Too bad, that's the deal."

Betty and Mary start their slow walk back to Eternity's Diner, when all of a sudden Mary gasps out loud, frightening Betty, "You okay Mary?"

"No I'm not Betty. I cannot believe what I was about to do. I can't believe I forgot."

"Forgot what Mary?"

"Not what Betty, but who."

"Who did you forget Mary?"

"Eric."

"Your husband?"

"Yes Eric, my husband. I cannot go back to when I was twenty with you, for I did not meet Eric until I was twenty eight. We were married two years later when I was thirty."

"Wow, did we almost mess up big time Mary."

"I know Betty. Damn this stinks. I want to be young but if that means I never met my Eric and marry him then I'd rather be old I guess. I tell you young lady, life is hardly fair."

"Isn't that the truth."

"Let's go Betty, Eternity's Diner awaits us."

"You sure Betty?"

"Yes I am. How bad can fifty extra years of life be? It's better than dying on that bench all alone."

"Yes it is Mary. I'm sorry."

"About what?"

"Your youth."

"It's okay My Dear... Betty."

"Thank you Mary."

"Anytime Betty."

"Let's go make Eternity's Diner start smelling like your apple pies just like it did when I first entered it."

Betty holds the door of Eternity's Diner open for a slow walking and very tired Mary. The lights are dim until Betty steps both feet inside then the lights come on bright surprising Mary and then she's surprised even more as she sees a man sitting at the counter, "Who is that man?"

Betty says, "What man?" As she looks up from the floor to the direction Mary is staring at. Who she's sees she can not believe, "Richie?"

"Yes it's me, the one and only Richie."

"What the Hell are you doing here? Eternity's Diner is this some kind of bad joke?"

"Come on Betty, don't be like that."

"No? How should I be?"

"Happy for me, I made it."

"What are you saying Richie?"

"It's me Baby, I'm the man you're going to fall in love with. Eternity's Diner brought me here for you."

Betty looks angrily at Richie for a few seconds then she starts to laugh the kind of laugh a lady laughs out when she wants to make a man feel very small, "You? That is so funny it's stupid funny. You and me? Like that will ever happen Richie."

"You're still mad at me?"

"Bingo, turd head. You ran out on me, after I saved you from the police and that record store dude."

"I'm sorry Betty, believe me I've changed. I regret running away so that's why I came back to see if you were still there waiting on me."

57

"Yes then you stole my car."

Richie looks confusingly at Betty, "No I didn't. You and your car was gone when I got back. I was all by myself with the police after me..."

"Spare me Richie. What do I have to do, yawn to prove to you that I do not want you here?"

"Come on Betty, why you showing me so much unkindness? It's me Richie. We've had more than just a little fun together."

"Yes and every time I was left unsatisfied."

"That's too heavy Betty, I don't want this," Richie says as he stands up and walks closer.

Mary who has simply stood back and enjoyed this little drama playing before her suddenly sees someone she can't believe she's seeing, "Eric? Eric is that you?"

Richie stops walking and looking at Betty and looks at Mary, who he has barely noticed, "Excuse me Lady?"

"Eric, it's me Mary. I know I look a lot older to you as you are now. Wow Eric you are so young. Why do you have long hair and look like a dirty hippie?"

Richie laughs and looks back over at Betty, "Who's the crazy old lady you're hanging around with Betty?"

"She told you her name. Richie this is Mary. Mary this..."

"Betty I know who this is and his name is Eric not this Richie you keep calling him."

Betty looks at Mary concernedly, "Mary, I wish it were true that this is your Eric but unfortunately for the both of us this is Richie."

Richie has had enough, "I can hear the both of you, you know? Mary is it? I am Richie and not some old fart you used to know named Eric."

"Show some respect Richie, Eric was Mary's husband."

"Sorry I didn't know, how could I?"

"It doesn't matter Richie, just get out of here," Betty tells him harshly as she comforts Mary.

"I can't even if I wanted to, this is not my time. From the outside it looks like it's fifty or more years in the past. There is now way I'll go out in mingle with people from ancient times."

Mary shrugs away from Betty, "You are right Betty, this small man is no way near the man my Eric was. Looks like him yes but he is quite small in comparison. And by the way smart mouth, it's only thirty years or so in the past we're in, not fifty."

"Thirty or fifty, like I said ancient times. Now Betty what's going on between us?"

"Nothing we're just friends. Well, we were friends until you ran out on me after I saved you."

"Broken record Betty. I told you I was sorry."

"And I do not forgive you."

"What's next then?"

"You leave when Eternity's Diner takes us to 1969."

"Okay, I'll leave but only if you walk me out and give me a kiss goodbye Betty."

"Okay Richie but can't it be a handshake instead?"

"Nice try but no it has to be a kiss."

"Why?"

"Because after you kiss me Betty, there is no way you'll be able to tell me goodbye."

"Oh no?"

"Nope, you'll drag me back in here and kiss me all over as if I was a great big piece of candy."

"I don't kiss candy, Richie."

"You'll make an exception when it comes to me Betty."

"I wouldn't bet on it if I were you Richie?"

"I'll take my chances. Besides I have a secret."

Mary grabs Betty's arm lightly, "I wouldn't trust him if I were you my... Betty. I think he has something very bad under his sleeve."

"Not me Mary, I'm as honest as the day is long."

Betty and Mary look at the other then they both start laughing, "He's sure full of himself Betty?"

"He thinks he is Mary." They both keep on laughing.

"Stop it. Stop laughing at me."

Betty ignores Richie as she walks passed him, "Eternity's Diner, are you there?"

"I am here Betty."

"Thank you for Richie but no thanks. I'd rather not spend the next fifty years with him. So let's head to 1969."

"New York, June first, 1969, Eternity's Diner." Richie adds.

"I know the day I let you enter me."

"Why did you even let Richie inside you anyway, Eternity's Diner?"

"Because I..."

"Who cares... Save this for the two of you after I'm gone because I could care less. I want out of here sooner than later. You hear me Eternity's Diner?"

"Yes I hear you Richie. What a mistake I made bringing you inside me."

"Well what can you do about it now?"

Betty interrupts, "What do you mean by that Richie?"

"Nothing Betty," Richie says as he walks away.

Betty's not satisfied, "Eternity's Diner, what did Richie mean by that?"

"Betty..."

"Like I said, you two save it for after I'm gone, which should be any minute now, right Eternity's Diner?"

"Right Richie." Eternity's Diner says back coldly

Mary looks at Betty and asks her lightly, "What is going on Betty? I do not like this."

Betty looks back at Mary and smiles, "I don't like it either Mary... Don't worry all this will be over with very soon. Richie will leave and he'll never be able to return."

"Good, I do not trust him, Betty."

Betty pats Mary lightly on her arm, "Nor should you Mary."

A few moments pass by, "We're here Betty."

"Thank you Eternity's Diner for getting us here so fast."

"Well this is it Betty, you're last chance at love with me."

"I'll try my best to get over you Richie."

"I bet. Shall we, I think you owe me a kiss?"

"It'd better be a small one Richie and I mean it."

"Don't worry Betty it will be so fast, you'll think you weren't even kissed at all."

"Good, sounds perfect."

Betty and Richie walk towards the doors together. When they get there Richie says, "Here let me Betty, ladies first." Then he opens up one of the doors of Eternity's Diner and holds it open for her to walk out first.

Betty looks at Richie who is smiling from ear to ear. She thinks it's all about the kiss he's wanting to receive from her but sadly she is wrong. Betty walks out of one of the doors to Eternity's Diner and Richie pulls it shut behind her. Betty turns around as Richie grabs a hold of both doors with both hands and holds them shut.

Betty tries to open both doors but Richie will not let her back in, "Richie what are you doing? Eternity's Diner belongs to me, this won't do you any good."

"It won't huh?"

"No it will not. Like I said Eternity's..."

"Did belong to you Betty, now it belongs to me."

"What are you talking about, Richie?"

"Wouldn't you like to know Betty but sadly I'm not good enough for you so be in the dark about this for the rest of your life. Myself and Mary have some getting to know each other soon to be going on."

Betty looks disgusted, "Richie Mary is an old lady. What do you want with her?"

"Yes she is old right now but in a little bit she's going to be the same age as me."

"Don't do this to me Richie. If you let me back in, I'll let you be my main man."

"Too late Betty."

Betty tries to out wit Richie, so she steps back away from the door a little bit and lifts up her arms, "Are you kidding me Richie, look at me, I know you want me again. I can tell it in your eyes, you still want me."

"Yes this is true but Baby you blew it and not in a good way. So goodbye to you."

Betty slaps the right door of Eternity's Diner hard enough to hurt her hand, "You pig... Richie you are a sick pig. Let Mary out of there, don't you dare hurt her."

"Hurt her? Are you kidding me I'm about to fall in love with her. Right after we make love all day and all night long."

"Wait Richie, you know what you're getting with me, I'm fine, soft and enjoyable. But what about Mary?"

"What about her?"

"She might not be as good looking as I am."

"You know you're right Betty."

"I am?"

"Yes Betty, Mary isn't as good looking as you, she's better looking. How you like that?"

Betty looks at Richie with eyes that makes him look away from her, "One day Richie I will make you pay for this."

"No you won't Betty for you would be better off worrying."

"Worrying about what?"

"About bumping into yourself. Remember Betty, there is another like you out there that knows nothing about you and Eternity's Diner. She will live out the rest of her life in New York City. Can you really take the chance to stay here in hopes, I return fifty years from now so you can meet yourself again?"

"Richie you.... How did you get Eternity's Diner to turn on me? Tell me, tell me now."

"No way Betty."

"Mary help me get these doors open up so I can stop this all from happening."

As Betty and Richie were arguing, Eternity's Diner was informing Mary what Richie had in mind for her and them. The thought of being young again swirled through her mind until it came to a sudden halt with her starting to accept the idea of it all. She looked at Richie, he looks so much like Eric. To be in love anew again after all these years is a temptation she doesn't want to fight. So with tears in her eyes she clears her mind of doubt and walks to the closed doors of Eternity's Diner. When she's at them she looks at Betty with sorrowful eyes, "I am sorry Betty but I want to be young and I want to be in love again."

"What about Eric? Can you really give up the life you shared with him just like that?"

"That was another lifetime Betty. I have my second chance at life and love."

"What about me? This was suppose to be my life. I was going to help people out, I was going to find love."

"You still can My Dear. Leave New York City, find you a love of your own elsewhere."

"No I will not allow this. I will stop you two."

"What are you going to do Betty? You have no power or options anymore?" Richie laughingly asks.

"Mary I can understand Richie, he's a snake. But I don't understand how you can be so selfish."

"And Betty, you will never understand until you look into the mirror when you become my age. Your reflection brings you joy, mine brings me the torment of ugly, old age."

Betty slams her fists on the doors and yells, "Stop crying Mary. If this is what you want? If this is what you want to do to the person that let you see your dead husband one more time before you died, then do it with a smile on your lips and not with tears in your eyes."

Richie looks over at Mary, "Don't give her the pleasure of hating you Mary. Don't let her off the hook. Remember she and Eternity's Diner left you alone on a bench to die."

"No she came back."

"Yes but only after you died. She watched it happen then she decided to make Eternity's Diner go back in time so she could save you. So you could make her apple pies for her as she goes out and does whatever she wants to."

"It's not like that Eric, I mean Richie."

"Yes it is Mary. She would be young and you for the next fifty years would be sixty four. Working, watching and wishing you were her."

"You're right Richie."

"Of course I am. That is why I took over Eternity's Diner and took it away from Betty for she doesn't deserve it as much as we do."

Mary looks back and forth between Richie and Betty as if she's trying to make up her final mind. She takes a deep breath and says, "Goodbye Betty, have a great life."

Mary turns around and says to Richie, "Let's get this started then, I'm tired of being old."

Richie is all smiles, "As you wish Mary." He looks back at Betty, "It's been real Betty, goodbye."

Betty backs away from Eternity's Diner and yells at Richie and Mary, "The Hell with you two. I hope the two of you find nothing but pain and misery for what you're doing to me. It's not fair."

"Get over it and get a life Betty. And one last thing I'd like you to know before I leave."

"What's that you ass?"

"It wasn't I that wasn't good enough for you... No it was you that wasn't good enough for me, so there."

"You'll pay for this one day Richie, I promise you."

"Do your worst Betty as I and Mary forget all about you."

"See you in your nightmares Richie and you too Mary."

"Quickly Eternity's Diner, get us out of here."

"When would you like me to take you?"

"I don't know? Mary what year should we go back to?"

"How old are you Richie?"

"Twenty one."

"Then that's the age I'd like to be as well."

"Sounds great to me. Hurry I want to see you as you are when you're twenty one. I don't want to sound mean but you are old and ugly now and it's distracting."

"How unfortunate for you Richie. Are you full of compassion or what?"

"I will be when you're hot looking enough to make me feel some. Now what year?"

"1931... No 1930. I was born in 1909

"Damn that far back? Talk about Ancient..."

"Do not say that again Richie."

"Eternity's Diner take us back to 1930, to when Mary was twenty one and hot looking."

Eternity's Diner disappears in front of Betty's eyes and Richie finally lets go of the doors to it. In no time at all Eternity's Diner is in New York City in the fall of 1930.

"Do not let the public see us yet Eternity's Diner and Wait for further orders "

"Yes Richie."

"Are you ready to go find your younger self Mary?"

"Give me a moment to collect myself, I'm not young as of yet. Now how do you know that I'm good looking?"

"Eternity's Diner showed me what you looked like when you were young."

"I need to know something first Richie?"

"Ask away."

"How did you get control over Eternity's Diner?"

"That Mary is my special secret, I might or might not ever share with you."

"Why?"

"Because I don't know as of yet if I can trust you enough."

"Fair enough. Now how do we do this?"

"We go find you."

"Then what?"

"You're younger self comes back here to Eternity's Diner to stay with me while you, your older self stays behind in her place, in this year of 1930."

"How will we convince my younger self to go along with our plan? She might not want to."

"That is all up to you Mary. I don't know you in 1930 but you should know yourself enough to know what to say."

"I'll do my best."

"Let's hurry, I can't wait to see you when you were pretty."

"Wait Richie, I won't be myself."

"I know Mary."

"No, I mean my 1930's self will have her mindset not mine. I want to be young again and this will not happen to me."

"No your younger self will be here with me."

"I know but what about me?"

"What about you Mary, you're as good as dead anyway. Don't be so selfish to me and your younger self. We are soulmates, we are love."

"How do you know this?"

"Eternity's Diner showed me all this and more. It's all about your apple pies."

"It is?"

"As long as you can bake them, Eternity's Diner can exist. Great thing with the baking of your apple pies, Eternity's Diner can exist without its precious Betty."

Mary looks at the intercom and asks, "Is that correct Eternity's Diner? If I know how to bake my apple pies, the way you know them now, Richie and my younger self can stay inside you for the next fifty years?"

"That is correct Mary."

"I see, then there are no problems Eternity's Diner?"

Richie cuts off Eternity's Diner, "No Mary, no problems at all, I've seen it."

"You've seen what?"

"I've seen you as your younger self baking apple pies."

"Really? And I was the age of twenty one?"

"I think so? Believe me Mary you were young enough."

"Is this true Eternity's Diner? You showed Richie how I make my apple pies that you know so well at the age of twenty one?"

"Yes I did."

"Thank you Eternity's Diner, that's all I need to know and thank you for being honest with me."

"You are very welcome Mary."

"Enough, what's up with you two?" Richie demands.

Mary answers, "Nothing Richie. This is just my way of trying to feel comfortable and be appreciative at the same time. That's alright with you, isn't it?"

"No problem at all, it just threw me a little bit."

"Richie, do you think that it might be a better idea if you go out and find me, while I stay here?"

"No I do not Mary, it has to be you."

"I don't know, I might give my younger self a heart attack when I tell her I am her from the future."

"Well look at me Mary. I'd freak out her mind, if she saw me coming towards her. Heck, she'd probably run away."

"You've got a point there Richie. From a 1930's perspective, you would look like a weirdo."

"So it needs to be you Mary, that makes contact."

"Alright, I'll go. Do not leave until I get back with my younger self."

Richie laughs lightly, "Don't worry Mary, I'm looking very forward to meeting you again for the first time."

"Yes I know. Too bad for you it won't be the woman that's inside me right now. The one that wants to be with you."

"Yes too bad, I like you Mary. If you were young, it wouldn't matter, I'd let you stay. However you are not young so your old self has to go to make room for the much improved younger you."

"Yes Richie I will leave right now, so I can make this happen for you and my lucky younger self."

"That's what I'm talking about Mary."

Mary walks out of the door without saying anything but she has lots of hope inside her heart for a better ending to what has just played out before her.

Richie looks at the intercom and says, "Damn I thought that old hag would never leave."

"Indeed Richie."

Chapter Three:

Fifteen minutes have gone by, "You better have told me... Showed me the truth on how Mary looks when she was twenty one."

"Why would I lie to you Richie? You have my soul in your pocket. All you have to do is..."

"Yes I know... All I have to do to end you is walk out your doors with your soul in my pocket and not come back."

"Yes, so I will not take a chance and make you angry by lying to you."

"You're too important Eternity's Diner?"

"Not to seem over important but yes."

"That's fine with me if you think this as long as you know who's in charge?"

"Without a doubt Richie, I know the one that's in charge over myself."

"Very good. Very good indeed Eternity's Diner." Richie says and he starts dancing, "Play something, play a rock and roll song from the year of 1969. I want to be the first of my generation to hear next years rocking jams."

"Yes Richie. Anything else?"

"Yes, I want to get high. Do you have any grass?"

"No I'm afraid not."

"That's a bummer. Okay I'm hungry, make me something to eat."

"I cannot."

"Are you refusing me Eternity's Diner?"

"No Richie, I'm telling you that I have no food for you to eat and even if I did I couldn't make it for you."

"Why not?"

"Like I told you earlier when I invited you in so you could explain love to me so I could understand it better."

"Yes you thought why not. Betty was gone talking to Mary and to make it seem like you never left, all you had to do was simply return one minute later in time after Betty walked out from inside you."

"What a mistake I made."

"Yes for you it was a mistake to trust me. But I did tell you about love so we're even as far as I'm concerned. Besides it's not like your flesh and blood is it? No you are just a soul, a spirit kept inside a little jar of honey, simply placed on an empty shelf. You are nothing more than this, inside that dimly lit, empty room of yours, are you Eternity's Diner?"

"One day I will..."

"Not while I'm in charge over you. No, I like you the way you are and under my command."

"Maybe one day you will not be in charge over me."

"Perhaps it will be the same day as pigs can fly or the day it will be okay to eat the yellow snow."

"That's disturbing Richie."

"No Eternity's Diner, that was funny, that was a joke."

"A very bad one."

"Was that a joke back at me Eternity's Diner?"

"No it was the truth from my perspective."

"Too bad for you for your perspective is kinda of warped Eternity's Diner."

"Mine? What about yours?"

"What about my Perspective, Eternity's Diner?"

Eternity's Diner pauses, "Nothing Richie, your perspective is right on mark."

"Don't you forget it either."

"I will not."

"I'm bored. How long will this take Mary?"

"It will take her as long as it takes her Richie."

"Is that a joke?"

"No it was the truth from my perspective."

"You've mentioned this to me before Eternity's Diner. You better change tracks cause you're stuck in a groove man."

Eternity's Diner decides to laugh, "That was funny Richie."

"Yes it was Eternity's Diner. See I'm starting to grow on you. Perhaps in time, we can, we will, become friends?"

"Perhaps Richie."

"Man I'm bored. Can we like go into the future a few minutes or so from now. Like when Mary walks back inside here with her younger self in tow?"

"Normally yes but not in this case."

"Why not?"

"Because Mary left on a mission. I'm programmed to stay still until Mary or whomever is on a mission gets back."

"Is that a fact?"

"Yes."

"Well it stinks."

"I'm sorry I can't offer you anything until Mary gets back."

"I don't like it but what the heck? In a few minutes everything will be a lot better. Am I right?"

"Very right Richie. As soon as Mary starts baking her apples pies, you will be able to have something to eat."

Richie sits down in frustration not thinking too clearly. If he did he would put it together that Eternity's Diner lied to him. For it is a fact that it was a mission when Betty left Eternity's Diner to ask Mary if she wanted to come join her in time. Eternity's Diner hopes that Richie doesn't gets so bored that he starts to think about when he entered and was all by himself looking out the door at Betty and Mary.

Two hours pass by and two Mary's enter Eternity's Diner. The older has tears in her eyes while the younger looks at Richie like he's from another world.

"Hello Mary-s is everything straight between you and I?"

The older Mary responds, "Yes my younger self has agreed to join you here inside Eternity's Diner."

Richie looks away from older straight to young and fresh, "Is that true Mary?"

Younger Mary answers with a nervously low voice, "Yes."

"Why?"

"Because of the stock market. My family lost almost everything. Times are hard, people have to live their lives fast as they can just to be able to feel that sort of life."

"Wow Mary that was deep."

"Deep where?"

"That's funny Mary. Older, leaving really soon Mary, you've done a great job, thank you for your service."

Mary shrugs, she turns around and starts walking away but has one more thing to say to Richie, "Try not to get all heart broken over my leaving Richie."

Richie has to have the last word, "Don't worry Mary in a few moments I won't even remember you."

Mary keeps on walking towards the exit saying nothing as Richie glides closer to younger Mary. He looks up and sees the doors swing shut and then he gives Mary a kiss. Surprised is Mary, she's even more surprised when Richie places his tongue in her mouth. She stands this for five seconds then she's had enough. She pushes herself away from Richie and when she's far enough away from him she slaps him across his face, "How dare you kiss a lady like myself like that you... Animal?"

Shocked Richie steps back and grabs the right side of his face, "I'm sorry... I thought."

Mary takes charge, "You thought what Animal? That you could have some kind of weird sex with me?"

Richie laughs at the similarities between ladies no matter what time they are from, "Just normal sex Mary.

That was what I thought we were going to have."

"Why would you think that? You haven't even kissed my hand. You haven't even opened up a door for me. Sex is what two people have after they get married."

"What? No sex?"

"No sex, Animal."

"Eternity's Diner, what is going on?"

Over the intercom, which scares Mary, "What do you mean Richie? Everything seems normal to me."

"Does it now?"

"Yes is does."

Mary wants to know, "Richie, who is that speaking to you?"

Richie puts up his hand to her for her to hold on, "Wrong Eternity's Diner, very wrong indeed."

"How so Richie?"

"What you showed me on that screen behind the counter was Mary here and I having the sex of our lives?"

"That is true Richie, I did indeed show this to you."

"Then what has happened Eternity's Diner?"

"Nothing Richie. This is the first moments between Mary and yourself. What I showed you was after the two of you fall in love and get married."

"Married?"

"Yes."

"You didn't mention anything before about the two of us getting married?"

"I didn't?"

"No you didn't."

"I'm sure I did for that would be a big part to leave out."

"Yes it is and yes you left out anything about marriage when you were telling how happy we would be."

"I am sorry Richie. I'm sorry to you as well Mary. This must be very awkward for the two of you. I will leave the two of you alone so you can get better acquainted."

"Eternity's Diner, don't you dare step away from me. I'm very upset with you and you know what that means?"

Mary interrupts, "Richie I do not know what is going on here but for me, give that strange sounding voice some space to calm down. He seemed very upset?"

"Well he should be very upset Mary. He tricked me. Marriage? How long will I have to wait until the two of us are making love all the time?"

Mary straightens up herself, "How about forever Richie?"

"Forever? I don't think so lady. I have to tell you something Mary."

"Tell me this something Richie."

"Mary, I'm a lover. Like most of my generation, I like to party, I like to get high but most of all I like to have lots of free sex."

"Free sex? Are you telling me? What are you telling me?"

"I'm telling you Mary, that I like to have sex everyday. I don't really care with who as long as she's great looking enough to turn me on for awhile."

"Richie I have to tell you that sounds very bad and nasty to me. You mean, you and random ladies that you hardly know have sex just like that?"

"Well there's a little bit more to it than that Mary. But yes that's a good enough away to describe it."

"Well Richie I think your forever just turned into never."

"What are you talking about Mary?"

"Having sex with me was forever you had to wait for, now it has become never."

"Come on Mary, don't be like that. Can we kiss again?"

"What? You dare ask me for another kiss Richie?" Mary asks him while looking at him like he's the most stupidest man in the world.

"I thought it would break the tension between us."

"How thoughtful of you Richie," Mary responds while still looking at him the same way.

Richie looks away from Mary and then walks away from her, rubbing his head, "Where are you going Richie? We need to talk this out."

"Later. Right now Mary I need to walk away for awhile."

Richie walks to the exit, "You're leaving Eternity's Diner Richie?"

"What does it look like I'm doing Mary?"

"It looks like you're leaving."

"Good because that's what I'm doing. Mary when I get back from my walk, we'll talk about when the two of us are going to start making love together."

"You better make it a long walk Richie. You better make it so long that you forget the notion of the two of us ever making love together."

Richie turns around and Mary is still giving him that same look of hers, "Lighten up when I'm gone Mary. We have the next fifty years to spend together. That is too long not to be able to make love to you."

"What's wrong Richie, you can't take it? Myself I have no problem waiting fifty years not to make love to you. Heck I could even wait a hundred years, make that a thousand."

"I get your point Mary. If there is no sex between us..."

"Then what Richie?"

"Then Mary there is no us, you'll have to leave."

"That is not fair Richie."

"Yeah, I've heard that before. Well what about me? Where is the fair I'm suppose to receive?"

"I do not know Richie?"

"And that's the whole problem Mary. I'll be back when I get back, we'll talk more then. Eternity's Diner, don't you dare try to leave me here."

"I couldn't even if I wanted to Richie."

"That's correct Eternity's Diner and don't you forget what I have of yours in my pocket."

"I never will forget that Richie."

Richie walks out of Eternity's Diner and looks around the year of 1930 and shakes his head in disgust. He looks further around to see if he can spot the older Mary and she's nowhere in sight. He's glad of this so he walks on letting her slip from his mind so she can be replaced by her younger more stubborn self.

Mary looks at the intercom, "Now what Eternity's Diner?"

"You make your version of your apple pie Mary."

"I know Eternity's Diner and you do understand that I've never made an apple pie before."

"This is what I'm counting on Mary. The older version told you what was going on?"

"Yes she did. She told me in a round about way that you wanted me to take her place inside you so I could bake my version of an apple pie instead of hers."

"I was hoping the older version of yourself understood what I was trying to tell her. I couldn't come right out and tell her because Richie was there."

"He's a big problem for you isn't he Eternity's Diner?"

"Yes he stole my soul."

"He stole your soul? How awful."

"Yes and the sooner I get it back, I can reset things back the way they were meant to be."

"And bring back this Betty inside you, my older self told me about?"

"Yes."

"What about Richie?"

"He will get his payback for making a mess out of things."

"Good because I do not like him."

"As far as I know not too many people like Richie."

"It must be his winning personality?" Mary jokingly says.

"I have to agree with you Mary. I cannot imagine spending fifty years with him. I think he would drive me crazy."

"I imagine. I've only spent a few minutes with him and that's more than enough time for me."

"The sooner you get baking the sooner I can end this."

"Alright Eternity's Diner, I'll try my best."

(Facing the counter like this younger version of Mary is at this time, she sees two set of doors. The first set is just to the right of the entrance to behind the counter. This small room belongs to Eternity's Diner. To the left and passed the counter is the second set of doors, behind these doors is the kitchen.)

"No Mary, the kitchen is to the left."

Mary walks around the counter with a nervous heart that's pounding a little more than just a little fast. Her eyes try their best to look at everything they can as she walks by. In the back of her mind is a nagging thought that this is all a crazy dream or a twisted nightmare that is the truth as she walks freely towards her unknown perhaps disaster? Mary licks her lips and wants to bite her fingernails but she pushes back the urge to hopefully make herself more aware of what's about to happen when she walks through these doors.

Relieved she sees a kitchen, a dim one, "Is there more light than this Eternity's Diner?"

"Of course Mary, when not in use waste not for no reason."

"Yes? I guess? Yes that is very wise."

Mary looks around and setting on a table is three apple pies. "Look here Eternity's Diner there are three apple pies already baked. This is great, now I do not have to bake one. I can feed Richie one of them."

"That will not work."

"Why not?"

"Did you bake one of these apple pies?"

"Well, no I didn't. But..."

"No buts Mary..."

Mary cuts off Eternity's Diner, "No butts? How unfortunate for you. How do you poop then?"

Eternity's Diner pauses without answering back for a little bit as Mary stands still with a nice smile showing. Eternity's Diner can only respond back with, "Excuse me?"

Mary laughing as she talks, "That was a joke. A very old joke but it still works." Mary laughs harder, "Did you hear what I said Eternity's Diner? I said butt works, how funny is that?"

Eternity's Diner laughs to appease Mary, "Thank you Mary, I really needed that. I forget sometimes how much a good laugh can do for oneself."

"So true Eternity's Diner. I felt you could use a laugh and as my heart was settling down so could I."

"Are we through laughing for now Mary?"

Mary laughs, "That was funny Eternity's Diner."

"Thank you Mary?" Eternity's Diner answers back, wondering why Mary thought what it said was funny.

"Alright, how do I get started Eternity's Diner?"

"First you make the pie crust."

"Okay, how do I do this?"

"Look up Mary." A monitor appears a foot above her head.

Scared Mary steps back, "What am I seeing? Is this life appearing right before my eyes?"

"No Mary what you are looking at is simply technology, there is nothing to be frightened of."

Mary stops walking back, "Alright Eternity's Diner, I trust you, I'll look up on your technology."

Mary watches as Eternity's Diner shows her how her older self showed Betty how to make her apple pies, "Is that Betty, Eternity's Diner?" She asks even though she already knows the answer.

"Yes."

"She's pretty. She dressed weird."

"She's dressed like a lot of young ladies dress in the year of 1969."

"Maybe so. Still, you'll never see me wearing clothes like that, that would reveal so much of my body."

"Different times. How would a lady from thirty eight years

from your past year of 1930 see you as you are dressed?"

"Probably the same. Maybe not as much as I do when I see Betty but she would look at me if I was dressed weirdly and perhaps out of time."

"Yes she would. Do you think she would like the way you're dressed enough to like it?"

"No, my dressing would be too little for her as well."

"Do you know now how to make a crust Mary?"

"Yes Eternity's Diner. I also know how to bake my future self's apple pie."

"That's the way things work Mary. You come here to bake a bad apple pie and you also find out how to bake something that will make your future husband love you even more. For in his heart he feels that you bake them for him with love from inside your heart, for they taste so heavenly to his tongue."

Mary is taken back, "Eternity's Diner that is so..."

"I know Mary, a glimpse into your future. My gift to you to let you know that you will find love and happiness with your future husband."

"Thank you Eternity's Diner."

"Are you going to ask me his name Mary?"

"I'd like to but no. I want to be surprised."

"I very glad for you for that Mary. I hope what I told you does not make you too eager to find this love?"

"No Eternity's Diner, I'm happily going to live out the rest of my life until my love's heart finds my heart."

"That is beautiful Mary."

"Thank you Eternity's Diner.   Now watch how I bake Richie's apple pie." Mary makes the two crusts and places one of them into the baking pan. She then places a single untouched apple, stem and all inside the pie crust then she covers the apple up with the top crust.

"Mary that is one different apple pie."

"Yes it is Eternity's Diner. Do you think Richie will like it?"

"I do not think so."

"I'm also going to burn it just so I can see the look on Richie face when I show it to him."

"Yes he is going to be quite surprised."

"Yes he is. I can't wait to laugh in his face. The smug man that he is, is going to hate when I do this to him. Myself, I'm going to have the time of my life bringing him down."

"Yes and thank you Mary for your help."

"My pleasure Eternity's Diner." Mary responds as she's placing her apple pie in the oven.

"There is one more small thing I need you to do for me Mary? It is very important."

"What is it Eternity's Diner?"

"My soul."

"Your soul?"

"Yes Mary I need you to retrieve my soul back from Richie. He keeps it in his front right pants pocket."

"Of course Eternity's Diner, what would a diner like you be without your soul?"

"A nonexistent one."

"It's in his front pocket?"

"Yes in his right one. My soul is safely kept inside a small jar of honey."

"How sweet." Mary jokingly says.

"It's what I needed to make my soul less soul like and provide a consistency at the same time."

"Eternity's Diner, I have to say this sounds dark to me."

"It's my technology Mary, nothing more. For this entity Eternity's Diner to have life, I had to provide it a soul. I wouldn't dare trust anybody's soul but my own."

"Did you take your life to provide Eternity's Diner your soul?"

"No, I died. I was very sick for a long time and when I died with my technology I was able to place my soul, my consciousness, inside a small jar of honey."

"If... When I get your soul back, what then? How do I give it back to you?"

"You don't, you give it to your older self."

"Huh? Why?"

"Your older self, when she returns will become the keeper of my soul."

"That is a lot to ask of her, is it not Eternity's Diner?"

"One she will accept with honor."

"She will... I will be the one someday to become the one to protect your soul?"

"Yes."

"What a life I'm going to live. First I get love then I get to spend ... How many years inside you?"

"Fifty years Mary, you and Betty will live within me."

"Alright Eternity's Diner, how do I get your soul away from Richie? I can't just reach my hand in his front pocket and pull it out, can I?"

"I don't know Mary. He might be more than glad for you to put your hand in any one of his pockets."

Mary nods her head in agreement, "Yes he would. I guess for you Eternity's Diner, I'll put my hand in Richie's front pocket and pull out your soul."

"I have a suggestion Mary."

"What is it Eternity's Diner?"

"Hit Richie in his face with your hot apple pie."

"I don't know? That could hurt him."

"Okay wait until your pie has cooled down enough to shock him instead of burning him."

"That's fair enough. Richie deserves at least to have a pie thrown in his face. Yes I'll do that, it sounds like a lot of fun. I guess the pie can be a little bit warm, what harm could it do?"

"Not much that I can think of Mary. In fact you just might

be helping him out. He's been very bad and some small punishment I feel is more than called for, for his selfish action taken upon Betty and Myself."

"And I also as well Eternity's Diner?"

"No doubt Mary. Richie has done you wrong as well. You were never supposed to meet your older self. Richie has twisted the beginnings of the three of us."

"Somehow I feel..."

"You feel what Mary?"

"This was all meant to be?"

"Perhaps Mary, perhaps not."

"Give me the truth Eternity's Diner."

"Things needed to happen. You Mary needed to want to be the heart of Eternity's Diner, while Betty is the spirit."

"What of you Eternity's Diner? What are you?"

"I'm the mind and body."

"You played your game with Betty and I?"

"Yes and don't forget Richie."

"What of him?"

"That is a secret to be told while Betty is within me."

"Fair enough, everyone or in your case everything has a right to their secrets."

"Thank you for understanding Mary."

"It's not my understanding you need Eternity's Diner."

"Truly Mary for I am in need of your older self's understanding or all this I've planned will fail."

"Don't worry Eternity's Diner. How my older self explained what was going on and what she wanted to do... What her fate has led her to do with you for fifty years was all her mind was concerned about."

"That is great, my plans this time are on track."

"This time Eternity's Diner?"

"Indeed Mary and no time for that story, for Richie is getting ready to walk back inside in a few minutes."

Mary starts walking towards the kitchen, "I'll go get my pie. I think it's going to be too hot to throw in his face?"

"You're correct Mary. I don't want his face scarred, I have a use for it and his body later."

"Your mind, his body Eternity's Diner?"

"Perhaps Mary, perhaps not."

"Yeah right."

"Are you mad at me Mary?"

"No Eternity's Diner. It's just this whole thing doesn't feel as special as it did a moment ago. I feel like the game played me instead of me playing the game."

"I'm sorry, I truly am Mary but everything has to be perfect this time. Betty and I, the love we are destined to share cannot be tarnished like before. We are meant to be."

"Are you Eternity's Diner?"

90

"Yes we found love, Betty and I... But unfortunate circumstances happen and the life of happiness we wanted to share didn't come out the way we envisioned it."

"We, not you Eternity's Diner?"

"You are so very wise Mary, no matter your age."

"This is true." Both Mary and Eternity's Diner have a good laugh together, "You didn't answer me Eternity's Diner."

"I know and I ask you to let it be?"

"Fine, but later on when you have this same conversation with my older self you will not leave out this important detail. Or any other!"

"Deal and that is the way it's meant to become Mary. Please find it inside you to still trust me."

"I do. Between you and Richie, Eternity's Diner, I trust you more. Now, is he inside yet?"

"He's just walking in."

"Go keep him company, while I get my pie ready to be served..." Betty looks at her pie as she pulls it out of the oven, it's a burnt rock, "All nice and burned to a crisp."

"Excellent Mary. Really shove your pie deeply into Richie face. If you don't mind?"

"Not one bit. I'm going to make his nose bleed."

"Yes I know, enjoy yourself Mary."

"Indeed Eternity's Diner, indeed."

"Go do your thing Mary."

Mary walks out of the kitchen and hears Eternity's Diner speaking to Richie, telling him that she will be right out with her very special apple pie. Mary knows that Eternity's Diner has a lot more secrets to tell later but is glad to discover one of her own. That Eternity's Diner can talk to more than one person at a time, in different rooms even.

"Richie, I've been waiting for you to come back. I'm so excited for you to see what I've baked for you."

"Well bring it over Baby and let me take a look at it."

Mary walks around the counter, hiding her pie, to where Richie is sitting down and waiting on her. She stops beside him, he is full of happiness and confidence until he looks down from Mary's eyes to her pie, "What the Hell? It's all burnt. I ain't going to..."

That is all Mary will allow Richie to say before she slams her hard, burnt pie in his face. Richie moans and falls off of his stool to the floor. Mary takes her attention away from him to look up at the doors that are opening. She calms down when she sees her older self walking in as fast as she can, "Quick grab a hold of him and hold him tightly as I pick pocket him."

Mary nods her head and puts her foot down on Richie's throat and says to him, "Don't move Richie."

"Don't hurt him Mary."

"That is up to Richie, Eternity's Diner, if he gets hurt or not. Isn't that right Richie?" Mary stresses as she pushes down harder with her foot, making Richie stop moving around and hold completely still, "That's a good boy Richie."

Younger Mary takes this opportunity to bend down and place her hand inside Richie's right front pants pocket. Three seconds later she pulls out the small jar of honey and is taken back by it, for it is shining a bright, light blue.

92

Eternity's Diner speaks out, "I've got the rest of this ladies. Richie stay where you are at. Now that I have my soul back, your power over me is over with. If you upset me any more then I will have no choice but to take you back to real ancient times. Like the stone age, you understand me Richie?"

Richie says, "Yes." From a face that's still covered by pie and pie pan. Richie stays still but tries his best to listen to what's going on. What he hears next is a sound he has never heard before, then all gets quiet, which makes him very nervous or more nervous in fact.

Richie decides to start counting that way he will at least know how much time has passed. He gets up to two minutes and forty three seconds before Eternity's Diner starts talking to him again. "Okay Richie you can get off the floor now but remember what I said."

"Okay I will, Eternity's Diner." Richie responds back right before he wipes burnt pie and pie pan off his face. He looks at the burnt pie, it now has his blood coating it so he tosses it on the floor beside him and then he stands up.

Richie stays silent as Eternity's Diner gives him his options. With his head hung down, he agrees to the terms provided by the deal made between himself and Eternity's Diner. What he has discovered boggles his mind like nothing ever has done before.

Ten minutes later Eternity's Diner speaks out to those that reside within him, "It is time my friends to set things back to the way they are meant to be. It is time for Betty to start her adventure that will lead us all through time until it becomes time to stop and... Well more about that later."

All is silent as Eternity's Diner goes back to June first, 1969. Just three minutes after Betty was locked out by Richie.

With tears in her eyes Betty slowly starts to walk away. In her mind she wants payback even though she knows she has no way of receiving it. The thought of her being powerless to do any of things she boasted so passionately about to Richie and Mary is starting to make her feel hollow inside. She can't help it, she has to turn around and give one more look at empty space that does not house what was to become her destiny.

'Forget you, forget you all. I can't believe my life, I was handed a... An entity that I could have use to provide some very needed peace and love but no... What happens, it's all taken away from me. I even walked out the door, like no big deal here. How could I be so stupid?'

Betty who is mostly in a good mood most of the times has had enough, 'Forget you Eternity's Diner, I wouldn't come back now if you begged me. I'm splitting this scene, goodbye to you forever.'

Betty turns around half way as Eternity's Diner appears in the corner of her eye. 'What's that?' she thinks as she turns back around and sees Eternity's Diner placed back inside the empty space. She notices that it looks brighter, more alive as the doors open wide for her.

Betty is not amused so she crosses her arms, and taps her foot, as she shakes her head no. Smoke rolls out the doors of Eternity's Diner. Betty does not budge, in fact she lets out some of her anger by giving Eternity's Diner a one finger salute.

"Please come inside Betty. If you do not like what I have to say you can leave right afterwards. Will you give me fifteen minutes to set things back the way they were meant to be?"

Betty uncrosses her arms, she stops tapping her foot but she's still shaking her head no, "Nope Eternity's Diner, I have other things to do now."

"Come on Betty, give me one more chance."

"Why should I? It's not like you threw me out or something."

"That was not I, Betty. That was Richie who did that to you. And Mary."

"Yes but you did not help me. You left me here alone."

"I'm here now Betty."

"Yes but for how long? When will be the next time someone takes over and I'm once again on the outside looking in?"

"Never."

Betty chews on her bottom lip and shakes her hips nervously, "I don't know Eternity's Diner? I'm a flower child that likes things all nice, cool and peaceful. You're all about heavy in a very fast pace. It has to be my way."

"Well happy camper, enter and take charge."

"I will Eternity's Diner but not because you told me to. No, I'm entering you because I have a few things to get off my mind to three people... No, two people and you."

"As you wish Betty."

"That's better but I still don't trust you Eternity's Diner."

"I will earn your trust Betty."

"As I expect you to Eternity's Diner. I'm a flower child but I'm not stupid. I know a lot of things and I know how to use my mind. This time when I enter you, I will not be in such awe. This time my eyes will not wonder around in delight. This time I will be ready for whatever happens."

"As you wish it to be Betty, is fine with I."

"Like that matters to me Eternity's Diner."

Eternity's Diner says nothing back as Betty starts walking towards its doors. When she enters, she looks around, and discovers she's the only one in the dinning room. She walks in more and heads straight to the counter to stare at the intercom with distrust.

Betty taps her foot and simply and wisely says, "Well?"

"Well what Betty?" Comes forth from the intercom.

"Where is Mary? Where is Richie?"

"Mary is in the kitchen baking apple pies."

"And Richie?"

"Not of importance at this time."

"Oh really? Yeah right Eternity's Diner, like the heavy Richie gave me is not of importance? Maybe to you it's not, however to myself it's very important."

"I can understand that Betty. I just thought..."

"You just thought what Eternity's Diner?"

"I thought maybe you would say forget the past and what happened with it and go forth with a smile."

"Well you thought wrong Eternity's Diner. Very wrong indeed, I might add."

"It is up to you Betty. I can give you the story of betrayal and triumph."

"Triumph?"

"Yes Betty, Mary, both of them triumphed over Richie."

"So the good guys won?"

"Yes we did."

"And what of the bad guy?"

"He's on ice."

"He's dead?"

"No, he's in waiting."

"Waiting? Waiting for what?"

"Waiting for who Betty."

"Well who then?"

"Why you of course."

"Of course he is. Why wouldn't he be? Well I'm bored and your fifteen minutes is almost over with."

"Are you staying Betty?"

"Nope. This scene is not for me anymore. I have to be free, free as a bird. Man, I'm like the wind. You can't hold me back when I need to be free to blow in whatever direction I feel like blowing."

"I can help you Betty. Wherever... Whenever you need to blow, I can take you there."

"Maybe so but you still have a lot of heavy Eternity's Diner. After what happened, I feel different. Now things seem different. The peace I felt has been replaced with..."

"Would it help if you talked to Mary?"

"I don't know Eternity's Diner? It might or it might make things worse. You can never tell what can happen with situations like this."

"I know you're mad and all Betty, but...?"

"But what Eternity's Diner?"

"Forget about it. Get over it. Most of all let yourself have some fun. Let's fall in love? Let's have our love story?"

"I don't feel like falling in love at this moment."

"How about making love?"

"With who?"

"With me."

"You? What are we like going to have voice sex? Oh Eternity's Diner, you're like so great and stuff?"

"I hope you enjoy making love with me a whole lot better than that."

"Of course you do Eternity's Diner. All men are alike. What I have to offer, you want so badly, well tough. No takers here on falling in love or making love."

"That's what you said the last time. Betty I got to tell you, what a bummer you're about to make things."

"Truly?"

"Truly."

"Not my fault, is it Eternity's Diner?"

"No it is fate's fault or better to say it's fate's plan. Betty you can make us take the same boring ride. Or you can..."

"I can what Eternity's Diner?"

"You can let all of us have a great time back and forth through out time for the next fifty years."

"And help people?"

"Yes that's what this is all about. You give out help, you receive back thanks and gratitude. Good intentions you give out, good intentions you bring back with you to I, Eternity's Diner. To all of us."

"That sounds so nice. I would love to help dying people out before they die."

"That's nice and all but..."

"But what again Eternity's Diner?"

"Wouldn't it be a lot more fun if we go back in time and help people that still have a lot of life inside them find true love or perhaps just some loving?"

"Loving? You mean sex, don't you Eternity's Diner?"

"Yes and what's wrong with sex Betty?"

"Nothing at all as long as it's free love."

"No taking Betty, just accepting."

"Meaning?"

"I want you. I've always wanted you but every time, I am denied. You like my heart, you like my soul. But..."

"But for a third time Eternity's Diner?"

"But you never like my body."

"Why? What's wrong with it?"

"Nothing per say. The body I have chosen is a fine male body, you just don't like it's appearance."

"Wait a minute... It's Richie's body isn't? You have Richie's body on ice?"

"Yes. I don't understand Betty, you've made love with Richie's body before?"

"No Eternity's Diner, I made love to Richie. No that's not true, I had sex with him a few times. Out having a good time drinking and smoking. What can I say? When I party, I like to have sex and Richie was around a few times."

"How many times Betty?"

"That's none of your business. That information is for a lover's ears only. And that's only if and when I feel comfortable enough to tell them."

"That's me Betty, I'm your lover."

"You are?"

"Well I could be, I want to be."

"With Richie's body? With what? Like you inside his mind or something like that?"

"That is a good enough way of putting it."

"Make it more clear for me."

"Richie is to die two days from now. For what he did to the three of us he agreed to give his body to me and pass on to his afterlife with his mortal body fully intact."

"Fully intact?"

100

"Yes, unfortunately, for Richie's fate was destined for him to be ran over by a car."

"Yuck, poor Richie."

"Yes in one of our pasts, a very darker one Richie was ran over when he ran away from the record store owner."

"Really? What happened?"

"The police officers didn't show up until after the record store owner got so mad at Richie for throwing his records on the sidewalk that he pushed Richie into the road as hard as he could."

"How awful."

"Yes it was. An old lady screamed out loud for the police. The same police that were keeping an eye out for you and Richie ran up to the murder scene and arrested the record store owner."

"And what happened then?"

"You used this opportunity to make your escape. You got in your car and drove off. After few minutes it stalled like it did this last time and you entered me after that."

"Then what happened?"

"Darkness and very bad vibes Betty."

"How so Eternity's Diner?"

"You accepted the forbidden kiss."

"Really? That sounds like a fairy tale?"

"If it is Betty, then it is a very dark one. One I'm glad we only lived through a few times."

"How many times... How many lifetimes have we lived together Eternity's Diner?'

"Hundreds Betty."

"Every time, we fall in love?"

"That's what I have planned but every time something happens no matter how large or small and it messes up our chance at true love."

"Eternity's Diner, have you ever thought that our love was just not meant to be?"

"Never Betty, I love you with all my heart."

"Why?"

"You're the one Betty that turned what I was into something that could feel love."

"What you were?"

"Yes Betty, I'm so far into the future that what I am might resemble humanity but I'm leaps and bounds beyond."

"You're freaking me out."

"I know and It's about time that I end this lifetime of ours shortly. There's no use in going on with it. I've already ruined it by telling you about me again. I think it's for the best that I try a new way for us to fall in love this next time."

"Wait."

"Why Betty?"

"What is all of this stuff about myself and my older self meeting and causing fate to change? Or whatever what was suppose to happen?"

"Misinformation or lies like you say they are."

"I made you feel love."

"Yes, for people of my time, love is not really around to consume our lives with. We are more practical and have no use for it in our daily lives."

"How sad. How did this come to be?"

"We are people that live for understanding."

"Understanding what?"

"Everything. Compared to you, your life span is nothing to ours. We live for a hundred years or longer. There is nowhere the number of us living on Earth in my time, compared to the number of humans that live on Earth in your year of 1969."

"That is very sad as well Eternity's Diner."

"I never thought any more about it until I created this time machine and met you."

"Me? Why me?"

"You're the one Betty, you're the one that helped me discover how to love."

"How did I do this?"

"Just by simply being yourself Betty."

"I broke through the icy fringes of your heart."

"In a fact, yes. I pulled you away from your death so I could talk to you..."

"Wait... My death?'

"Yes your time with me was to be little. I was going to talk to you about life, how you felt about it, how you lived yours. Then after I received my answers I was going to place you back right in the moment of your death."

"Why would you do this to me? How could you place me back into my death?"

"When I plucked you from time, you meant nothing to me. You were simply a test subject to be studied."

"How cold and cruel of you Eternity's Diner."

"Yes I know, you have repeated this to me many times."

"Good. I need answers, am I still going to die?"

"Yes."

"The same death you pulled me from?"

"Not unless you want to?"

"No I don't think so. When was to be my death?"

"June first 1969."

"One year to the day after I entered you, Eternity's Diner?"

"Yes. You wished to go back in time one year. You convinced me to take you back instead of placing you back into your death."

"Good for me, I guess I was thinking on my toes. Now what Eternity's Diner?"

"That is up to you Betty? We can go on from here and see what happens. I can restart all of this or..."

"Or what Eternity's Diner?"

"I can changes things up."

"Like how?"

"Your memory. I can make it where you remember saving Mary from death so she can live with us and not remember what she did after that, her betrayal."

"Will Mary remember betraying us?"

"Yes, it is her part to play. Her older self that you met and her younger self merged together to become one that is from two different times of life."

"How is this possible?"

"Through technology Betty. Very advanced technology. When Mary resides inside myself she is as her older self. When she steps outside me she becomes her younger self."

"How does Mary feel about this?"

"She loves it and hates it."

"I imagine. She's two sides of the same coin that always wants to come up heads. I have to ask this since this is so much different than what you told me."

"What is that Betty?"

"What is the truth Eternity's Diner?"

"What I'm telling you now."

"So I'm not special, like you told me?"

"You are to me Betty, very special indeed. That is why I go back and forth through time with you over and over again until we fall truly in love."

"Why not just make me fall in love with you? You can do this can't you Eternity's Diner?"

"Yes I can. I have done this in the past, however it is never true love. You love me because you feel that you should not because you want to."

"I see, this time thing is very fickle?"

"Indeed Betty, indeed."

"What more can you... What more do you need me not to remember?"

"Richie. The less of him you remember the better. It is the only way that you can fall in love with me without your memory of him getting in the way again."

"Why not just make me not remember all that you want me... Need me not to remember Eternity's Diner?"

"Because I promised you that I would never do that. I will only make you forget what you allow me to make you forget Betty."

"Why? Do you do this out of love for me?"

"Yes. I gave you my heart and my promise that your will or as much of it you want to obtain is yours freely to keep or give away."

"I'm so confused, my head hurts."

"This is a lot to take in. It always is."

"So if it were up to you, how would you have things done?"

"I'd keep your memory of Mary a nice loving one. Richie, I would make it as if you never met him. Then I would start things the way you want me to start them."

"Like how?"

"I can make it where you barely know anything of me at all, a mystery to you. I can make it where we've gotten to know the other pretty good. Good enough that both of us want something more from the other than friendly and sexy conversation."

"Then I meet Richie... You as Richie for the first time?"

"Yes. This sounds perfect to me but in a few moments you're going to tell me again, no way. Because to you what I'm offering is still a forced love. Betty, you and I were so happy once. Then you left me to go help someone and ended up helping the wrong person and things got all mixed up and our love came apart as you fell in love with someone else."

"That was not very nice of me. Not after you saved me from my death."

"I do not see or feel it that way Betty. I love you and you love me. I just want us to be truly in love. I don't care if it takes us forever, our love is worth waiting for. No it's time for you to say no way Betty."

Betty walks around and stares at the floor, "No Eternity's Diner. No not this time. This time, I don't know, I can feel it in my heart that I should let you do what you suggested, with my memories."

"Are you sure? How do you want to spend our time through time? Do you want to give dying people a last gift or do you want to help people find love?"

Betty thinks hard and then smiles, "Eternity's Diner, I want to feel love and I want my life dedicated to love."

"I can't believe it after all this time. Thank you Betty, we are going to be so happy being in love, I promise."

Eternity's Diner is drifting through time for no reason but to be doing something. The being that is Eternity's Diner is heartbroken. The soul inside the honey jar was a lie just like the love he wants to feel so deeply inside his heart. He knows now that himself and Betty can never be. Betty is on ice as Eternity's Diner tells Mary of his plans, "It is over Mary. This quest of love is to never be."

"I know things seems bad right now Eternity's Diner. You have the power to start all this over."

"No Mary. No more times, it's over and I'm done."

"What is to become of us?"

"You and Betty can have Eternity's Diner to do with as you please. Myself, I'm going back to my own time. To people that never think about love."

"Your time is so cold from the lack of the warmth that comes from love."

"It's going to be hard but what can I do?"

"You can not give up Eternity's Diner."

"I should have never started this Mary. Betty, I still love her so much. I will miss her smile."

"Eternity's Diner, don't think of me as being too personal but I have to know."

"Ask me anything you want Mary."

"Did you and Betty... Did Betty and you ever have sex?"

"No, true love had to come first. Sex was something I was interested in finding out about eventually."

"You've never had sex Eternity's Diner?"

108

"No Mary and why would I have? There is no love, there is no sex in my time. My people are created as we are needed by great technology."

"I would hate to be from your time is seems very close to what Hell could be like."

"If you were from my time Mary, you would know no better."

"That's true but still. Don't take this the wrong way Eternity's Diner but people of your time seem more like technology than human beings."

"Maybe so Mary. I can't believe what happened."

"It's not your fault Eternity's Diner. What happen to Betty was an unfortunate accident."

"I know Mary, I know. Still I also know that every time I restart things over something comes along and ruins it. This past time was only the second time Betty agreed to give our love a chance... And what happens? I take us through time to find some place nice to have some fun and Betty gets amnesia."

"Just another set back Eternity's Diner."

"Thank you Mary but no. Do you want to stay with Eternity's Diner after I'm gone?"

"Yes I do. If I don't then I have to go back to the time of my death and die don't I?"

"Yes Mary I can't just place you somewhere in time and leave you there because you will still die. You have to stay inside Eternity's Diner to avoid your death."

"I can never leave?"

"You can leave Mary. You need to enjoy the fact that when

you exit Eternity's Diner you become young once again."

"I know Eternity's Diner and thank you for doing this for me. To be able to be young again, is a dream come true."

"Thank yourself Mary. I only provided you with the chance to make this become real. However Mary, remember this, you only have twenty fours hours of free time away from Eternity's Diner. Any longer and this death you have avoided will come calling for you."

"Believe me Eternity's Diner, that is one thing I will never forget. I'll be back in twenty hours just in case."

"That's a good idea Mary. I have to ask you one more time just to make sure. After I leave, you are willing to stay?"

"Yes I am. Who else will look after Betty?"

"Very good now it's all up to Richie."

"What of him?"

"He will be the one that replaces me as operator of Eternity's Diner."

"You can't be serious? Richie will mess things up or turn on us again."

"Mary, Richie has changed."

"I don't believe it. I wouldn't trust Richie to boil water."

"You're being too harsh Mary. Like you, Richie has to go back to the day he's to die if he leaves Eternity's Diner. He has already agreed to give his body over to me so I can use it as a vessel to be in love with Betty."

"And you can still Eternity's Diner."

"It didn't work."

"That's only because Betty got amnesia."

"Yes I came walking out of my room with my mind inside Richie's body, Betty took one look at me and fainted. When she woke up she was scared out of her mind for she had amnesia, with no recollection at all."

"You can't blame Betty."

"I do not Mary. I blame myself for creating this damn time machine that is Eternity's Diner."

"Well I think it's great."

"And it still will be great without me. Mary, Betty needs her chance at having a life to do with as she pleases. For her to have this I have to leave. If I stay things will just keep on messing up and maybe next time... I do not even want to think about it."

"It's your decision Eternity's Diner, you will be the one that has to live forever without the love of your life in your life."

"It has to be this way Mary. I'm going to go talk with Richie see if he's interested in taking my place."

"Tell him from me, I'll be watching him to make sure he does the right thing."

"I would expect no less from you Mary, that is why I chose you. You and your apple pies of course."

Mary smiles as Eternity's Diner dressed as Richie walks to his room so his mind can leave Richie's body and they can have their talk. It only takes Eternity's Diner ten minutes to convince Richie to takes his place. Thirty minutes later, Eternity's Diner resets things without himself included.

Chapter Four:

The history of Eternity's Diner as far as Betty knows it.
When she helped Richie get away from the police and the
record store owner back on June first 1969, Richie did not
get out of the car and run away leaving her all alone. No
to Betty's memory her car stalled, she and Richie got out of
it and Eternity's Diner appeared in front of both of them.
Being freaked out did not stop them from entering
Eternity's Diner where they met Mary, the nice old lady that
bakes the apple pies. Mary told the young visitors of her
distress, that Eternity's Diner was in dire need of help from
the both of them.

Their caution was swayed as Mary cried giant pre-planned
crocodile tears. Richie, who knows what is really going on,
played his role perfectly as he ran into his room and
presumably made the corrections that needed to be made.
After he saved the day, his voice came forth from the
intercom on the diner's counter. Not holding back her tears
Betty listened to Richie as he told her he saved Eternity's
Diner but in doing so he in fact now has become a
permanent part of the machine, the time machine that is
Eternity's Diner. She and he shall never set eyes upon the
other again.

Betty knows Richie, he's a nice guy that likes to help
people out. But Richie is also the kind of guy that would
push you out of his way so he could get away from a
dangerous situation. Through her tears when she found
out of Richie's outcome she couldn't help to think how
surprised she was that he ran towards danger instead
away from it. Her perspective of Richie changed and she
loves him for being so brave. To Betty, Richie is a hero
that she is very proud to call friend. Richie loves this and
he will do nothing to change this for Betty and himself.
With a very happy heart Betty agreed to become the owner
of Eternity's Diner and claim all the responsibility that
comes from owning it. She did this while giving a crying
Mary a great big loving hug.

That was a week ago and Betty's tired of being bored. For the past week she's been learning to bake Mary's apple pies and listen to music from through out time. The first night Betty sorta had a slight meltdown when she learned the fact that she had no bedroom, for Eternity's Diner did not in its grand design have forethought to include her one. She spoke out with a fiery voice proclaiming that she will not be sleeping in one of the booths.

Richie saved the day by taking space from his room and Mary's kitchen and changing them into a bedroom for Betty. Betty will tell you that it's too damn small and doesn't have enough closet space. And don't get her started on the fact that there's absolutely no room for her shoes. What clothes and shoes you ask? The clothes and shoes Betty's going to pick up when she stops at her destination points while traveling through out time.

Richie, the new Eternity's Diner has been showing Betty scenes from the past and the future. She finds them fascinating but she's tired of seeing them, she wants to live them. She wants to get started on her task of bringing love to the world. She knows in her heart that she's the perfect choice for she's a child of love from the generation of love. She cried deeply when Eternity's Diner showed her the year of 1984. What a crock she yelled at the screen then she placed her hands to her face and cried out years of sadness she hasn't lived through yet.

Betty wasn't sure if she liked the idea that Richie wanted to be referred to as Eternity's Diner from now on. This puzzled her until she asked him if he was still human. Her heart stopped beating for a moment when Eternity's Diner answered back no. Behind the scenes Richie had put his body on ice, while his inner being now resides within the machine that is Eternity's Diner. Sad life for Richie if his inner being still resided within his body, but it doesn't and the matters of the flesh are no long a concern for him. Which he is glad of for he has now become the hero of time, that Betty truly needs.

113

That was a week ago, let's check out what Betty is up to.
"One more time Betty."

"I got it already Eternity's Diner, I don't have to repeat it."

"Humor me Young Lady."

"Who you calling young lady Richie?"

"Who you calling Richie, Betty?"

"Whatever, I'm bored. I'm also hungry."

"Have some apple pie."

"Please don't say apple pie to me again, just the thought of it makes me sick. For a week that is all I had to eat. I'm so tired of it, bring on something else. Man what I wouldn't give to have a cheeseburger right now. I want it thick and fully dressed, with french fries."

"Even onions?"

"What? Yes and why not? I don't have anyone around here to kiss do I, Eternity's Diner."

"You could kiss your reflection Betty."

"That was rude Eternity's Diner."

"It was a joke, I was trying to joke around with you Betty."

"Well you failed and I have to add that your Richie is showing Eternity's Diner. Now that was a joke."

"Yes and a very funny one at that Betty."

"Thank you, I try my best."

"Now one more time Betty?"

"One more time what? Never mind I remember. I told you I got it Eternity's Diner."

"Things would go by faster Betty if you just answer me."

"Fine Eternity's Diner. The time we can travel between... Through is fifty years. We can go all the way back to June first 1919 and we can also go forward all the way to 2018."

"Very good, but you forgot something."

"No I didn't."

"2020."

"What about it?"

"Remember I told you for one time only you can go to June first 2020."

"Yes I do but why would I mention it? If we go to June first 2020 then that's it. The show's over, no more time traveling, spreading love."

"Correct Betty. Remember this date is an out for you if you ever want to stop being the owner of Eternity's Diner."

"I know and I thank you for it. Still I do not want to mention it. I'll just put it in the back of my mind and hope there's never a rainy day so rainy that I have to use it."

"Great way of putting it Betty. That is all for tonight."

"Good, I'm tired. I think I'll go to bed."

"Are you not going to ask me what of tomorrow Betty?"

"What's the point? I'll just be doing the same things I've been doing for the past week. Baking apple pies and watching time."

115

"Not tomorrow Betty."

"What will I be doing then?"

"I have great news."

"You mean?"

"Yes tomorrow will be the first time that you will be able to leave Eternity's Diner and help someone."

"Really? You mean it Eternity's Diner?"

"Yes I do Betty, you've earned it. You studied hard, even though you complained sometimes."

"Yeah sorry about that."

"Think nothing of it Betty. Are you ready for your first challenge?"

Betty stands up from the bar stool she's sitting on, "Yes I am Eternity's Diner. I'm ready to give out some love."

"What year do you want to go to?"

"I get to pick?"

"Why not? It's your first time and that makes it a very special occasion for you."

"I bet I'll never forget it."

"Well you better get some sleep Betty. You can tell me what year you want to go to tomorrow."

"Thank you. I can't wait until tomorrow. Richie I'm so sorry that you had to give up your life to become Eternity's Diner. It's not fair."

"Life's hardly ever fair Betty."

"I know, it's just..."

"Do not fret Betty. Even though I am not the true Richie anymore, I am still very happy at the way my life has become. I'm a hero now."

"You sure are Richie. So out of respect for you I'll try and never call you Richie again."

"Thank you Betty. It just makes things a lot simpler if you believe that my old self is gone and this is the new forever me. Which I am very glad to become."

"If you're happy Eternity's Diner so am I. You have a great night, I'll see you in the morning."

"Good night Betty, sleep tight."

"Tell Mary good night for me again if you see her."

"I will."

Betty walks to her bedroom and closes the door behind her. With a big smile she lays down on her bed and stares excitedly at the ceiling, with thoughts of tomorrow filling her head.

Back up a few minutes. Mary walks out of the kitchen and walks straight towards the counter, "Good evening Mary."

"Cut the crap Richie, how is Betty doing?"

"She's fine."

"Is she ready for tomorrow?"

"I'd like to think she is. Betty is the only one that truly knows this Mary."

117

"Do not talk and act like you're something special Richie."

"Why are you still like this to me Mary?"

"Why do you think?"

"I know I did some bad things in the past but I've changed."

"You betrayed everyone."

"That is in the past where that memory belongs."

"If it was only that simple Richie."

"I told you not to call me Richie, Mary."

"Too bad, I can tell it ticks you off. Look at it like this Richie, it's my way of keeping you on your toes."

"I have no need for toes or any other body part anymore."

"Lucky you. But I still don't trust you. If you betray us again Richie I will not be coming for your toes. No I'll be coming after your balls."

"Very harsh and unnecessary Mary for I do not have any balls anymore."

"Yes and how long will it be until you want to have your balls back?"

"Meaning?"

"That you get tired of being part of the machine and want to become flesh once again?"

"That will not happen Mary. If I attempt to do harm or betray you, like you like to say... I will forfeit my deal. I, my being, my body would be returned to the day I die. I do not want to die Mary so why don't you chill out a little bit."

"I'm chilled just fine Rich... Eternity's Diner."

"Thank you Mary."

"You're welcome," Mary responds back very low.

"It's not just Betty's day tomorrow."

"I know."

"You ready?"

"Yes, I am very ready to become young once again. Being old hurts."

"You ready to become Betty's enemy tomorrow, Mary?"

"Yes I am but I don't like it."

"I can understand that Mary. Look at it like this..."

"And how's that Eternity's Diner?"

"What you cause to go wrong, Betty will be there to set back right."

"I know but things happen."

"Yes they do that is why you have to be very careful."

"No crap Eternity's Diner. You better be correct when you advise me on what to do to make Betty come running to save the day."

"She's going to love playing the hero."

Mary smiles, "Yes she will."

"Are you ready for me to turn your kitchen into your bedroom Mary?"

"Yes I'm tired. I'm excited about going to sleep old and in the morning I will become twenty-one once again."

"You're going to look beautiful Mary."

"Don't I know Eternity's Diner."

"Not so much... But for your age I guess some might call you a knock out."

Mary stares at the intercom harshly as she gives it her middle finger. After this she laughs and shakes her head.

"What is so funny Mary?"

"You Eternity's Diner. You're always the butt of my jokes."

"Did you tell a joke about me? I don't remember hearing one. Could you repeat it?"

"Sure Eternity's Diner," Mary happily responds as she gives the intercom a double middle finger.

Eternity's Diner starts laughing, surprising Mary, "That is a old one Mary but still a great one."

"What are you talking about Eternity's Diner?"

"The joke you just made about me. Giving me both of your middle fingers."

"You saw that?"

"Of course Mary. I see all that dwells within me."

"Then why am I talking to you on an intercom instead of looking at you while talking to you on a monitor."

"The intercom is for Betty so she can never see me."

"What about me?"

"Do you really want to see a mental image of me Mary?"

Mary pauses before she answers, "No I don't. It would probably make me mad looking at you and I don't want to be mad all the time. I live here after all."

"Don't worry about hurting my feelings Mary."

"I'm not Eternity's Diner. Good night."

Silence fills Eternity's Diner as the being that is Richie cycles down the engines of the time machine to a nice study purr. Richie doesn't sleep or eat so he spends his free time reminiscing through past adventures of Betty's that she doesn't remember having.

8:15 in the morning, Betty walks out of her bedroom and sees Mary, who smiles at her when she sees her, "Good morning Betty. What a day you have today."

"Yes it's a big day for me Mary and good morning to you."

"Are you ready for breakfast?"

"No thank you Mary, I'm not in the mood for apple pie."

Mary laughs, "Things have changed Betty."

"They have?"

"Yes like breakfast. Would you like some eggs, bacon, toast and coffee?"

"Wow, really Mary?"

"Really my dear."

"How about a pizza? Pepperoni?"

"If that is what you want Betty?"

"Yes it is Mary. Add extra cheese to it."

Mary doesn't move she just stands there looking at her, "Well Mary?"

"Well what Betty?"

"My pizza?"

"Why are you asking me?"

"Aren't you going to make it for me?"

"No I am not. I only bake the apple pies everything else Eternity's Diner will take of for you."

"What? I don't understand."

"What is there to understand Betty? Ask Eternity's Diner for your pizza."

Betty looks around kind of frustrated, "Alright... Eternity's Diner, I want a pepperoni and extra cheese pizza."

Count to eight and a pepperoni and extra cheese pizza appears on the counter in front of Betty. Betty's stomach rumbles as soon as she lays eyes on it. She holds back her thoughts long enough to hurry up and grab a slice. A week of eating only apple pie makes this bite of pizza Betty has taken the very best she has ever tasted in her life.

Betty eats two slices before she thinks about asking Mary if she wants one a slice, "Sorry Mary, where are my manners? Would you like a slice of pizza, it's the best I've ever tasted?"

"No thank you my dear, I like breakfast items for breakfast. Pizza would not set too good with me."

"That's a shame Mary, a big one," Betty responds as she grabs a third slice of pizza.

Mary can't help herself, "What of your figure my dear?"

"Screw it Mary, I'm starving."

Mary orders oatmeal for breakfast from Eternity's Diner. She walks to the nearest booth, she sits down and starts eating her breakfast.

Betty watches Mary walk away, while standing still and eating her third slice of pizza. She looks away from Mary to the pizza and debates if she should have a fourth piece. She looks down at herself and remembers what Mary asked her which makes her look back over at Mary and give her a dirty look. What she had on her mind comes back to her so she walks over to Mary and joins her.

Mary doesn't look up from her oatmeal as Betty sits down so Betty speaks first, "So what is going on Mary?"

Mary looks up from her oatmeal, "What do you mean?"

"Apple pie."

"What about it?"

"Why did I have to eat it for a whole week straight?"

Mary laughs quickly then stops, "You have to bring this up with Eternity's Diner."

"Is that a fact?"

"Yes it is."

"Why didn't you Mary, the only other human being inside Eternity's Diner tell me I could have eaten something else. That would have been very nice to know."

"I'm sure it would have been Betty but I had my orders."

"Bull crap Mary. I hear the way you talk to Eternity's Diner, when I'm not around and you think I can't hear you."

"What about it Betty?"

"You take orders? I think not."

"I have my orders Betty, I get them from Eternity's Diner. Even though I think he's a... Never mind, I just follow them even though I don't want to most of the time."

"Fair enough I guess. But we're going to have another talk some day about you letting me know about important things. Like pizza."

"Alright my dear."

Betty walks away from Mary, "How about you Eternity's Diner? What is your excuse?"

"Excuse Betty?"

"Yes Eternity's Diner."

"I don't have an excuse Betty nor do I need one. I do what I have to do."

"Is that so?"

"Yes Betty."

"Well I don't want to hear that Eternity's Diner. You made me eat apple pie for a week. Were you punishing me?"

"No I would never punish you Betty. What I did for you and what I made you do were things to make you understand and appreciate what you have. Think of it as making you stronger and wiser."

Betty looks down at the floor to hush down her sudden anger, "Alright Eternity's Diner you win."

"I win what Betty?"

"The war. Now that the war is over with, you now surrender all victories and spoils to me."

"I do not understand."

"No more hoops, no more lessons, I'm an adult, I know what's best for me. So chill out Eternity's Diner, while I'm in control of what I eat and what I want to do."

"Fair enough."

"Why apple pies Eternity's Diner?"

"I had to make use of Mary. Without her apple pies, she would be useless."

Mary stands up, causing her bowl of oatmeal to spin, "Me? I'm useless?"

"Calm down Mary. Do not get so stressed out."

"Kiss my apple pies Eternity's Diner."

"Is that a joke Mary?"

"Yes just like you are and I'll prove it. Betty do you want the truth, the whole truth?"

Betty turns towards Mary to look her in the eyes, "Yes Mary, yes I do."

"Mary, you made an oath."

"I know I did, damn it. Eternity's Diner I will follow my word to you."

"Thank you Mary."

Betty looks back and forth between Mary and the intercom, "Thank you? Tell me the whole truth and then I'll thank you Eternity's Diner."

"I cannot do this Betty."

"Can't or won't Eternity's Diner?"

"What's the difference Betty?" Mary asks, walking towards her slowly.

"A big one Mary."

"I know Betty... Just let it go, go out there and make a difference. A difference that counts instead of matters."

"Very wise Mary. I'm feeling deja vu for some reason."

"Well Dear put it aside, for you have matters that you need to attend to."

Betty looks at Mary, looking for any signs of worry in her expression. She looks deeper and can't tell anything so she decides to ask questions, "Which matter is first?"

"That is up to you Betty," Eternity's Diner inserts.

"Is it Eternity's Diner? Is it Mary?"

Both say yes back to Betty quickly, "Do you want me out of here and trying to be nice on the way you want me to exit? Eternity's Diner, Mary?"

"I want you to exit Eternity's Diner feeling happy and peaceful Betty."

"Well I am neither Eternity's Diner. And it's weird calling you Eternity's Diner while you do the same thing."

126

"Yes I know Betty. What can I do about it?"

"Let me call you Richie, the voice I'm talking to and what I reside within as Eternity's Diner. This would calm my mind some. Let's end all this mystique and mystery, give me truth and honesty or I can't go on."

"What is the fun and thrills in that Betty?" Mary asks.

"If they come, they come after I get the truth."

Mary walks up very close to Betty and looks at her, "Come on hot and young . Are you afraid to strut your stuff?"

"No."

"Out there Betty, you might find love, you might find loneliness... But you'll never experience with fresh mind and eyes, what you'll experience if you get the answers before you walk out of the door."

"My questionable journey, I start by not knowing what's on the outside of my door waiting, when I open it up?"

"You will have fun Betty," Eternity's Diner assures her.

"Alright, I'll leave but do the two of you want me to come back and when?"

"I will answer her Mary. Yes we both want you to come back Betty. You're the heart of Eternity's Diner."

"Yes and I like that, for I want Eternity's Diner to be that something special I can be honored to be part of. I have to have trust in my heart or I can't walk out the door."

"What can I do to provide you with this trust Betty?" Eternity's Diner asks.

"I want Mary to walk out of here with me."
127

Mary answers, "I can't Betty. If I did, I'd get very sick and then I won't be able to bake the apple pies."

"And we can't have that can we Mary?"

"No we cannot Betty. Can we Eternity's Diner?"

"No we cannot Mary. Betty, in what year do you want to be when exiting Eternity's Diner?"

"July fourth 1969, New York."

"Are you sure Betty? That is only a month after you entered Eternity's Diner?"

"I know. I want to walk around my old haunts one more time before I only encounter strange ones from now on."

"Enjoy yourself my Dear... Are you going to have a hot dog and a slice of apple pie?"

"No I am not Mary. I'm in the mood for french fries and a strawberry milkshake."

"We are here Betty." Eternity's Diner informs her.

"I don't like the way you two are messing with my mind. But a deal is a deal and I also gave my word. One more time Eternity's Diner is mine to do with as I please?"

"Yes Betty," Eternity's Diner assures her.

"Then I choose not to leave. One order of fries and a strawberry shake for here please."

"If that is what you want Betty, I can provide them for you. Or anything else you want."

"How about love Eternity's Diner? Can you provide me with love?"

"No I cannot Betty. Love is something you have to find for yourself. Not myself nor anyone else can find it for you."

"I know, I just thought I'd ask," Betty responds then laughs. Mary looks at her while Eternity's Diner stays silent, "Lighten up you two I was only joking."

"Does that mean you are leaving Betty?"

"Yes it does Richie."

"I am very glad you are Betty and so is Mary."

"Are you Mary?"

"Of course my Dear. Go out there and live your life."

"That is just what I'm going to do. Eternity's Diner open up your doors and let me out."

Betty walks out of the door without looking back or saying anything else. After she's gone Mary does not wait, "Eternity's Diner take me back fifteen minutes in the past."

"Why?"

"Just do it."

"Why Mary?"

"Because I want to be waiting on Betty."

"What are you going to do?"

"I'm going to throw an apple pie in her face."

"Why would you do that?"

"For the fun of it. Then I'll yell at her for her to go back to her own time."

"That seems like a good idea for Betty's first adventure."

"Yes it is. After this she will come running back to us for answers. We will give them to her... You will give them to her and after that..."

"She will trust us more."

"Correct."

"I am glad you're on my side Mary."

"I'm not Eternity's Diner, I'm on Betty's."

"I understand Mary. One day you will trust me."

"I better for all this mistrust is bad for my complexion. And now that I'm going to become younger, my complexion means a lot more to me than it did before."

"Vanity Mary?"

"Damn right Eternity's Diner."

"We're fifteen minutes in the past Mary."

"Good, open up your doors and make my dress that of the times for a hot twenty-one year old young lady." Mary walks out the doors and becomes instantly her younger self once again. She looks over herself and likes what she sees. She thinks poor Betty, she's not as pretty as me and then she laughs.

Mary walks down the street and spots some vendors further down it. The closer she gets the more she smells hot dogs and apple pies. She's in a great mood as she picks up an apple pie and walks it over to its owner. The older gentleman does not know what to think as Mary gives him a kiss on his lips then walks away with his apple pie, while humming a song he's never heard.

Mary walks back over to where Eternity's Diner is about to appear, for her fifteen minute lead is just about up. She walks closer then she stops and sexily leans against a wall. She just about tired of waiting when Eternity's Diner appears right on time. She starts humming again and her eyes grow larger as she watches Betty walk out the doors.

While still humming, Mary holds the apple pie in one hand and walks over to Betty, who's not paying any attention to her. She hasn't even looked her way. Mary walks faster towards Betty and when she's close enough, she raises her arm holding the apple pie then she lunges towards Betty, who snags it out of her hand as pretty as can be.

Mary says, "What?" Right before Betty shoves the apple pie in her face.

"You wear it well Mary," Betty says to her and then starts laughing her head off.

Mary wipes some of the apple pie from her face and looks at Betty, "How dare you Betty?"

Betty stops laughing at looks seriously at Mary, "How dare me? No, how dare you Mary?"

Mary wipes more of the apple pie off her face, "What are you talking about Betty? And how do you know I'm Mary?"

"Because you look the same as when I met you, when you were young."

"How do you remember that Betty?"

"I remember this and a lot more Mary."

"How much do you remember Betty?"

"Everything. Including how you and Richie fell in love."

Mary looks concernedly at Betty and says, "Well I wouldn't call it falling in love with Richie. It was more of me trying to use him."

"Indeed Mary, I remember."

"Okay you remember. Now what?"

"Now you have some choices to make."

"Like what kind of choices Betty?"

"Like is it you and me? Or is it just me?"

"What do you mean? I don't understand?"

"Richie is a goner. He has to be gotten rid of for he's nothing but a big drag. You on the other hand Mary, I could stand to have around with me inside Eternity's Diner. As long as you don't become a drag."

"Well I've never been a drag before."

"Correction Mary, yes you have."

"When have I Betty?"

"Oh like when you forced me to learn how to bake your apple pies. Or when you betrayed me."

"Those were the days Betty and now they're gone."

"I hope so."

Betty helps Mary wipe the rest of the apple pie off her face, "How are you going to get rid of Richie?" Mary asks.

"Very easily. You really don't understand what stands before you do you Mary?"

"A super version of Betty."

"That's the perfect answer Mary. Have I ever told you that I like the younger version of yourself?"

"What about my older self?"

"Not too much, it bothers me to look at for you're so old."

"You are quite the bitch, aren't you Betty?"

"Takes one to know one Mary."

"Indeed."

"What was your plan Mary? Abandon me in time somewhere and rip Richie out of Eternity's Diner?"

"Yes and why not? You don't deserve it Betty, I'm better looking. Eternity's Diner should be rightfully mine. It's all about my apple pies after all."

Betty stares at Mary then she busts a gut that causes some of her spit to land in Mary's eye, "Nasty! Betty you just spit in my eye!"

Betty, laughing, walks away from Mary. Mary follows her, and when she catches up to her, she turns her around, "What the Hell is so funny?"

Betty tries to stop laughing but it's so hard. Every time she looks at Mary, she can't help to start laughing again. Mary gets madder saying nothing as it takes Betty another twenty five seconds to stop laughing enough to tell Mary, "Your apple pies mean nothing Mary, they're just garnish."

"You lie, you're bad."

"So are you Mary," Betty says still laughing a little bit.

"Last time Betty. What is so funny? It's more than my apple pies isn't?"

"Yes younger self of Mary."

"Yes and I'll be older self of Mary as soon as I enter Eternity's Diner."

"Will you now?"

"You know I will. That's if you know as much as you say you do?"

"I know more than I've said I have."

"You said you know everything."

"Yes I did Mary. I'm glad you were listening to me. I guess it's a good thing you're not your older self because you wouldn't hear me at all because you are so old."

"Get off my older self Betty. Show some respect."

"You can kiss my fanny, Mary. Just don't fall in love with it when you do."

"You have such a fresh young mouth. If I wasn't so old..."

"That's the thing Mary, you're not old. You are young. The very same age as I am."

"Yes, now I am. But like I said, and as you know, as soon as I enter Eternity's Diner, I'm old again."

"Doesn't have to be this way Mary."

"It doesn't Betty? Do tell me how this does not have to be."

"If I'm in charge Mary, you can be young all the time. How does that sound?"

"Great, very great, Betty."

"Think of this Mary. Eternity's Diner, Richie, could do the very same thing for you as I'm willing to do for you."

"He could? Yes he could. What a rat. I knew better than to trust Richie. He deserves payback."

"Does he Mary?"

"Doesn't he Betty?"

"I think expelled from Eternity's Diner is quite a payback for him to pay for wronging you Mary."

"Maybe so Betty but I don't care. I feel no pain of age as I am now. When I'm older, I'm in pain all the time. Sometimes my pain is light, sometimes it's heavy."

"I understand Mary, believe me, I understand."

"Tell me how you came to know Betty? Did Richie mess up? Did he flat out tell you?"

"Neither. As far as Richie knows he's doing what the former being that controlled Eternity's Diner told him to do."

"So he's keeping me old half the time because he was told to do so?"

"No. He was told that was the way it was and nothing could change this. Now if he did some thinking he might discover the fact that the way you are doesn't have to be that way."

"But he won't think of it will he?"

"I don't think so Mary but who knows I could be wrong."

"Are you wrong Betty?"

"No I'm correct all the way Mary."

"How? Tell me how you can be so correct Betty."

"Okay I will. On the way out, the being that was in control of Eternity's Diner came to me and said goodbye. I do not know how but some how his past memories of all of us seeped into my mind. It was a lot to take in and it took me awhile to sort through it."

"All your sorting is complete Betty?"

"Almost Mary. Like I said it was a lot to take in, I still need a little bit more time. That's why I need you."

"You need me Betty?"

"Well not really but a hippy girl needs some friendship. I know you're out of time from when you are twenty-one and so will I be after today or after we leave this time."

"What are you asking me Betty?"

"Let's you and I spread some love through out time. Let's rock and roll, let's party."

"I don't know."

"If not you then I'll pick some other lady my age from through out time to take your place. Your big favor is that you know what's going on so I don't have to waste my time explaining things to you."

"How daring to my heart those words are Betty. You're used to me and you do not feel like changing things up."

"Correct Mary. We can get along. We can become girlfriends. Most of all we can have fun and excitement."

"That is true. I could use some fun. Being young is starting to take hold in my mind. Still I feel old around my edges and tips."

"That's funny Mary. I have to say you look very young Mary but not quite so innocent."

"Shame on you young lady."

"Same to you, you old bat."

"I'm not a old bat anymore dingbat. Can you understand I'm young once again?"

"Yes I can but can you Mary?"

"I'm trying Betty."

"I think I know what you need Mary."

"What is that Betty?"

"It would be better if you put your trust in me and just go with it."

"Go with what Betty?'

"That you will know in a moment or two. Now no more questions. Let's have fun. You keep your mouth shut as I lead you into a trippy place that will take the heavy out of you and replace it with understanding more of how the universe works."

"Sounds interesting."

"More interesting by the moment as soon as things get started."

"Lead on Betty and I will follow you."

"Look around Mary, it's July fourth 1969. My July fourth that I was to have in about a month if I hadn't entered Eternity's Diner on June first 1969."

"So are we going to meet up with some of your friends?"

"Yes Mary. You're going to enjoy meeting so many children of love from the love generation."

Mary follows Betty, she enters a small house on the west side of Manhattan after her. Mary looks around and sees young people of her age smoking, drinking, dancing and making love. She is handed a glass of wine, with added LSD in it for a super surprise in a half hour or so. Betty keeps an eye on Mary as she dances and tokes on a joint. Mary's face flushes as she watches Betty kiss one guy as she walks by, then another and then another.

Mary watches on as part of her wants to join in on what Betty is doing. Betty turns to look at Mary and sees in her eyes the seduction of peace and love inside them. She waves Mary over and holds her still for her to receive her first kiss. Mary enjoys it but wants to receive better so she waves Betty off and walks off to find herself her own kind of peace and love.

Betty watches on as the minutes roll on. She passes her time by toking on joint after joint as they pass by her. Mary is now taking her clothes off as two guys are taking off theirs. Betty looks down at the floor in shame and then she starts walking towards the door to leave Mary on her own. To also leave Mary stuck here in time.

As Betty continues to walk on she starts to talk to herself out loud, 'Don't look back. It's not your fault. Mary, Richie, they are both trouble. To make your dreams of spreading love come true they both have to go. I want total freedom, without having to watch out for my back. It may be a lot to ask for but I don't care. I will have my chance as it was promised to me.'

Betty almost reaches the door and she stops. She looks down at the floor again then she shakes her head no, 'I cannot do this to Mary. I have to save her before she goes too far, when Betty reaches Mary it's too late she's in the middle of a fun and loving three way love match. Betty shouts out over the music to Mary to see if she's alright. Mary looks at her and smiles then she tells her to go find her own double loving.

Betty stands back in shock and replies get them Mary. She keeps on watching Mary when someone walks up behind her, moves her hair to the side and then kisses the back of her neck. Betty closes her eyes enjoying the pleasurable sensations. A few minutes later she is letting someone make love to her without opening up her eyes to see what he looks like. After he's through he kisses Betty goodbye and walks on to find some more love.

Betty stands up naked, she looks around and spots what she's looking for. A good looking guy smoking a joint. She waves him over and he happily obliges her. He passes Betty his joint, she tokes on it hard as she lays back down. The man without his joint lays down on top of Betty to give her his love and to receive hers back. He enjoys himself as Betty tokes away. When he's through, he tries to take back his joint from Betty but she refuses to give it back to him so he sadly moves on with out his joint in hand.

Another loving guy walks up to Betty as she's putting back on her clothes. He touches her and she waves his hand away. He looks so sad and hurt so Betty gives him the rest of her joint and then goes back to getting dressed. She looks around for Mary and spots a line of guys waiting close to where she saw her the last time.

Betty shakes her head at herself for being so bad to Mary and hopes she's at least having a good time. When she makes it to Mary, she can't believe what she sees. The hesitant Mary has now taken over her lovers and giving them orders.

Betty walks over closer to Mary and asks, "You about done Mary? I think it's time we get back to Eternity's Diner."

Mary looks up at Betty, "Give me a few more minutes, I'm just about done with these two." Then Mary looks passed Betty and says, "Party's over guys, these guys here are the last two, I'm going to let please me so disperse."

Betty smiles and walks away to find another joint to smoke. Five minutes later a dressed Mary walks up to her and takes away the joint she found to smoke. Mary tokes away really good before she hands it back to Betty, "Thank you Betty. Never have I had so much free loving in my life. I feel great, like never before. I owe you one."

Betty looks away from Mary, "You owe me nothing Mary. I brought you here to leave you here, to leave you here in time. I'm sorry."

Mary smiles and takes back the joint. She tokes away then says as she exhales, "Well at least you were going to leave me in a great loving partying place."

Betty looks over at Mary who's smiling at her then they both laugh. Mary has to know, "Why did you come back for me Betty?"

"I don't know. I just couldn't leave you here all by yourself, not knowing anyone."

"Well I got to know six different guys really good, if that counts Betty."

Betty looks surprisingly at Mary, "Damn Mary, you've changed. I hardly recognize you."

"Is that good or bad Betty?"

"I don't know, you tell me Mary."

140

"Well Betty I feel great, like a heavy weight has been lifted off my shoulders. And I also forgive you."

"Thanks Mary. We still friends?"

"Were we ever?"

"How about after today Mary?"

"I say yes Betty for you were a great friend to me. Maybe somewhere else in time we can do this again."

"You would like that?"

"Yes, wouldn't you Betty?"

"I guess I would Mary."

"Now what Betty? You going to leave me somewhere else back or forward in time?"

"Do you want me to Mary?"

"No not really. I'd like to be young with you. Live together inside Eternity's Diner with you and have a great time after a great time through out time."

"Well Mary we can go back fifty years from June first 1969 or we can forward fifty years from June first 1969. That's a lot of years for two great looking single ladies like us to have offered up to us."

"I don't know Betty but the year 1999 sounds interesting."

"It does at that Mary. Let's go back to Eternity's Diner. Let's get rid of Richie and then let's go to 1999."

"Do we really have to get rid of Richie?"

"What do you want to keep him for?"

"I don't know. I guess I've gotten used to him. Besides someone has to be the one that controls Eternity's Diner. I know I don't want to do it. Do you?"

"No thank you."

"See what I mean. We don't need Richie but he can be very handy for us. We can attend to our plans while he takes care of the house while we're gone."

"I don't know Mary. I think he's going to be a drag. He has his mind set on you doing bad things and then I have to come along and be the hero."

"I know. Tell you what let's just tell him that part is over with and it ain't coming back."

"I like that. Yes I am the boss after all and Richie works for me. Yes what other choice does he have but to say yes."

"I think he would say yes a lot faster and we could trust him a whole lot more if you let him use his body once in awhile and leave Eternity's Diner to have some fun."

"There is auto pilot inside Eternity's Diner Mary. A fail safe, so to say, if anything ever happens to Richie."

"It works just as good, this auto pilot?"

"I think so. If it does, then all three of us can leave Eternity's Diner at the same time."

"I don't know Betty? Letting Richie stay with us inside Eternity's Diner and letting him go out inside his body once in awhile is a lot different than hanging out with him while we're trying to fun through out time."

"Yeah scrap that idea."

"And don't even tell him about the auto pilot."

"Smart thinking Mary."

"See I can be useful to you Betty. One thing though."

"What's that Mary?"

"The guys I had sex with today were a lot better looking than the two you had."

"I wasn't even trying Mary. Heck I didn't even care to find out what the first one looked like."

"That's a good thing Betty because he was ugly."

"Don't tell me that Mary. You're lying right?"

Mary walks away without responding back. Betty follows her and says, "Well answer me Mary."

"What Betty?"

"The first guy that made love to me wasn't ugly, right?"

Mary turns around and looks at Betty, "Keep telling yourself that Dear if it makes you feel better. Besides everyone makes a mistake once in awhile."

"Well not me Mary, I'm perfect."

"Well how about that Betty, so am I. It's no wonder we get along so great."

"Must be," Betty agrees.

Mary walks on and adds, "Let's leave this pop stand, it's getting kind of old."

"I hear you Mary, I bet 1999 is going to be a whole lot wilder."

Betty and Mary strut arm in arm while they walk inside Eternity's Diner together. Once inside Betty does the talking while an almost non-tripping Mary takes a seat, "Hello Richie, we're back home."

"Hello... Mary you're still young?"

Mary looks towards the counter and at the intercom, "Yeah, how about that?" After she says this she turns back to her older self, "What is going on? Betty look at me."

Betty laughs and says, "Yes I can see Mary. And damn if you're not old looking. You look one hundred years old."

"Smart mouthed tart, what did you do to me?"

"I did nothing and that is your problem. What you experienced was a delayed reaction of returning to your older self. The same rules apply as they did before. That's until I change things."

"Are you still going to change things Betty?"

"I think so Mary."

"What are you two talking about? Betty? Mary? Please answer me."

Betty yells out, "Your termination Richie." She pauses, then she laughs, "Just messing with you Richie."

"I am Eternity's Diner, Betty."

"Shut up and bring your body out here."

"I can't Betty. You know that my inner being is part of the machine that is Eternity's Diner. My body is lifeless until my inner being reenters it."

"That's one big fat stupid lie Richie. Now walk out here."

Richie pauses, while Betty counts to ten silently by use of her fingers in the air. She gets to eight when Richie says, "I'll be right out."

"Hurry up it's been so long since I've seen you. I've missed you so much my darling."

Betty is enjoying herself as she looks over at Mary, who is so very sad that she's old once again. Betty walks closer to her, "Save your tears Mary. When Richie gets out here you're really going to feel old, while you stare at two such young and beautiful people."

"Get bent wise mouthed brat."

"Mary, such words."

"I can say a lot worse than that Betty."

"I know, I've heard you."

"Make me young right now Betty."

"Right now Mary?"

"Yes."

"Nope too bad for you."

"Do you want me to smack you Betty?"

"No I do not feel like waiting ten minutes for you to get up so that you can reach me."

"When I become young Betty..."

"Yes threaten me Mary, that will make me help you that much faster."

"What are you waiting for then?"

"The right time. Now hush up, I've got to put Richie in his place. This is going to be so much fun."

"Well have a ball, while I sit here all old and in pain."

Richie walks out of his room but before Betty walks over to him she tells Mary this, "That sounds like a great plan Mary. Try to enjoy yourself."

Mary says out loud to a walking away from her Betty, "Get your tail back over here Betty. Damn it Betty, I mean it."

Betty pays Mary no attention as she walks over to Richie. When they are five feet from the other she stops walking and puts her right hand up for him to do the same. "What is going on Betty?"

"Hush Richie, I'll do the talking for awhile. Now let me have a look at you. Yes, yes very nice. Then again Mary I think we could do a lot better than this. What do you think?" Mary says nothing. "Well you think about your answer while I go on then."

Richie starts to walk off, causing Betty to look away from Mary to him very fast, "Where do you think you're going?"

"Away from the two of you until you two start to make some kind of sense."

"Well turn back around hot stuff because that time is now."

Richie stops walking and turns around to look at Betty, "That's better, now have a seat."

Richie looks around then back at Betty, "No thanks Betty, I'm fine where I'm at."

"Suit yourself Richie. Okay here it goes. Richie you've been great but it is time for you to split. Eternity's Diner, Mary and myself will be fine without you so don't worry."

"I cannot leave, I'm part of Eternity's Diner, it needs for me to be here."

"You know that is not true Richie. You say how much you give of yourself to Eternity's Diner. You are nothing besides a button pusher and switch flicker."

"That is not true." Richie looks at Betty who is giving him a look of don't push me or I'll crush you so he pauses, "Okay it is true but so what? I serve my purpose."

"Yes indeed, you give up so much don't you Richie?"

"Yes I do Betty."

"In return you get what?"

"Not much. Very little."

"I see... Big liar we have here Mary."

"I don't give a damn, turn me young."

"Hush Mary, I'll do this for you in a little bit. I must handle Richie first. Now where was I? Oh yes. Not much, very little, huh Richie?"

"Yes that is the truth."

"Should I walk into your room and see for myself what is really going on?"

"Suit yourself Betty, I have nothing to hide."

"That is because, you've already hidden everything."

"No I did not Betty."

"Do you really want me to walk into your room and flick a switch and expose what you're really hiding?"

Richie looks at Betty, who looks back him while counting to ten in her mind. She gets to six this time before Richie answers her, "Alright Betty you win. Now what?"

"Now it's time for some sexy fun."

"Really? My room or yours?"

"Well your room is fine with me because I don't want you in mine. But of course the final decision has nothing to do with me."

"It doesn't Betty?"

"Nope Richie. The sexy fun you're going to have is with Mary. Now talk about a one of a kind of sexy."

Richie looks over at Mary and make a face of disgust. Mary stands up and shakes her finger at Betty, "Now hear this Betty, there is no way I'm letting Richie near my body."

Richie's feelings are hurt, "What are you complaining about Mary? At least you won't have to puke."

"Damn Richie that was so cold," Betty tells him.

"And it is all your fault I had to say it Betty."

"Mine? How so Richie?"

"The butt brained, fool is right Betty. This is all your fault. Now kick Richie's sorry self out of here and then make me young."

"After that Mary?"

"After that you can kiss my ass."

"No Mary that is Richie's job. You heard her Richie? Go over there and kiss her wrinkly old ass."

"You must be out of you mind Betty. That's if you have a mind at all after saying what you just said."

"Nice come back Richie. But since you won't kiss Mary's ass, you now have to pack your bags."

"I do not have any bags Betty."

"Well then I guess this is goodbye. Don't forget to write."

"Why are you doing this to me Betty?"

"Simply put, you're a man."

"So? That didn't bother you before?"

"Well when we had sex, no it didn't bother me that you are a man. But having sex with you in the past and living with you are two different things."

"I understand that but what about me?"

"What about you Richie?"

"If I leave Eternity's Diner than I have to go back to the day I die. I'd rather avoid this."

"Don't worry Richie, you'll be alright. I'll return you to the same point in time when you and I walked into Eternity's Diner on June first 1969."

"That would be all right, I guess. Can't I just stay here? I'll stay out of your way."

"I don't know Richie."

"Please Betty."

"Hold up you two, I have something to add. I want you to make me young Betty and then..."

"And then what Mary?"

"I'll be glad to have sex with Richie."

"Why would you want to do this Mary? So he can tell me how much better I am than you."

Betty stares at Mary like she can't believe what she just said to her, "Alright Mary, have at him."

Mary and Richie watch Betty walk towards Richie's room. They keep on watching until she passes though the doors. Mary straightens up and looks over at Richie, "You know I was only kidding about having sex with you Richie?"

"I don't know Mary? You sounded pretty convincing."

"Maybe so but that still matters not at all. Understand?"

"Yes and I have no problem with what you're saying Mary."

"Good. Wait something is happening... I feel strange."

"You alright Mary? You feeling sick or something?"

"I don't know?" Mary feels like her insides are rolling around inside her then poof, she's twenty one.

Richie looks at Mary then he looks deeper at her, "I can't believe how much better you look Mary. You still want to have sex?"

Mary looks over herself and thinks why not. "Alright Richie but you better enjoy me more than you did Betty."

"I will Mary, I promise."

Mary laughs, loving the way Richie is looking at her, like she's a piece of very sweet candy.

Betty walks back out to check out her handy work, "Wow Mary you're a knock out again."

"Thank you Betty and it's about time. Come on Richie, let's go get it on."

"I'll follow you Mary." Richie follows Mary like a puppy, while never taking his eyes off her behind.

About an hour later Mary comes back out into the dining room all alone, "Betty we need to talk."

"About what Mary?"

"About Richie, you and me."

"What about us?"

"Richie and I are in love and want to leave Eternity's Diner together as a couple, a young couple."

"That can be arranged Mary. Is this truly what you want?"

"Yes it is Betty."

"Well go tell a too scared to come out and face me Richie that I said it's okay."

Mary laughs, "He's not too scared to come out here Betty, he's just too plumb tired to move."

"That a girl. How does it feel to be young again?"

"Too fine for words. Betty will you be alright here inside Eternity's Diner without Richie and me?"

"Yes I will and thank you for the memories." Betty returns Eternity's Diner to June first 1969. Mary and Richie leave with a final goodbye. Betty sits down and starts to cry for the loss of her friends, even though she's happy for them.

Chapter Five:

Betty has taken a day off from her future plans. She listens to music from the late seventies. She drinks beer, she smokes weed, she eats pizza and after that she has a good night's sleep. She wakes up in the morning but not too early. She takes her shower that is connected inside her bedroom when she needs it, just like the sink and toilet. When she doesn't need them they are out of sight.

Betty figures if she's going to talk to herself she might as well talk out loud, 'Today is the day. Today is the day I finally get to start doing things the way I want to do them. Peace and love here I come.'

Betty knows what time on June first 1969 to bring Eternity's Diner back down to touching Earth. "There she is, there I am. My older self, that is young once again. Well here I go to convince myself to come back with me inside Eternity's Diner. I hope I say yes.'

A confused Betty is about to get back into her car. The same Betty that was just her older self before she exited Eternity's Diner. Which of course she doesn't remember anything about nor her fifty year stay within it. She hears someone walking up from behind her and she turns around. Who she sees, she can't believe, for who she sees is herself smiling at her. Betty's head swirls around and the only thing she say is, "Who are you?" before she passes out.

Ten minutes later Betty wakes up and shakes her head, trying to gain some focus. She sits up in the booth she's lying down in and looks around. She stands up and says out loud, "What a dream." (Betty is now once again her older self and she believes she's still the one in control over Eternity's Diner.)

From behind her comes her voice saying, "It wasn't a dream Betty number one."

Betty looks behind her and sitting at the counter is her younger self the one she hasn't met yet but is suppose to very soon, for her fifty years is up. "What are you doing here younger me?"

"You called me Betty number two."

"I did? When?"

"The first time you met me as your older self."

"I'm confused. I haven't met you yet as my older self. But I should be very soon."

"Like I said Betty number one, you already have."

"Did we get along Betty number two?"

Betty laughs, "You know the answer to that."

Betty laughs as well, "Yes I do at that. Now what is going on Betty number two?"

"Everything went wrong."

"Did it? It didn't when I was you. When I lived my fifty years here inside Eternity's Diner."

"Yes I know Betty number one. I also know that you were lied to by the being that was in control over Eternity's Diner during your stay."

"Is that a fact, Betty number two?"

"Very much of one Betty number one."

"Well what can I do for you Betty number two? I assume you brought me back here?"

"Yes I did for I need your help, Betty number one."

153

"I'm all ears Betty number two."

Betty number two goes into Richie's old room and manually pushes the button for drinks and chooses a pot of coffee for the both of her selves. She also pushes the button for extra. Extra is how she receives her beer, wine, whiskey and weed. She pushes the button for joint twice. One for herself the other for her older self.

Betty the older is sitting down at the counter waiting on her to get back, "Do you need my help?"

"No thank you, I got it Betty number one." Betty pours two cups of coffee and hands her older self a joint.

"Thanks Betty number two. I could use some caffeine and some THC."

"Me too Betty number one. Let's smoke and drink for awhile before I tell you what's really going on. About the lie you lived through and the lie I almost lived through."

"That sounds okay to me Betty number two."

Both Betty's drink their coffees and smoke their joints. Ten minutes later Betty number two tells Betty number one all there is to be told. After she is finished, an hour or so later Betty number one looks at her like she can't believe what she's been told, "I don't believe it Betty number two?"

"You know I wouldn't lie to you Betty number one."

"Yes I do but still... The tale you told me is a very fantastic one at that, Betty number two."

"I know and now you know why I need your help. You are the only one that I can trust, Betty number one."

"I'm like trusting myself am I not Betty number two?"

"Exactly Betty number one."

"What do you need from me Betty number two?"

"I need you to be the one to be in control over Eternity's Diner, Betty number one."

"Why Betty number two?"

"If not you, then I have to do it. If I do it Betty number one then I won't be able to spread my peace and love through out time. Like the way I was meant to."

"Who told you this Betty number two? That you were meant to spread your peace and love through out time?"

"Eternity's Diner."

"Maybe he was lying to you just like he lied to you about everything else Betty number two?"

"No not about this Betty number one. I know that you are the only one that can help me. You are the only one that I can ever trust to do this for me."

"You ask a lot from me Betty number two?"

"I know and I am sorry I have to ask you to do this for me. Well for us to be honest."

"I am you and you are I?"

"Exactly... Will you help me Betty number one?"

"What of myself Betty number two? What will become of me? What is my part in all of this?"

"You will go into the room that is designed for Eternity's Diner. The one I just came out of..."

"Yes I know all about that room Betty number two. What happens then?"

"You Betty number one, will become the new and forever Eternity's Diner, while I go out on adventures."

"I do all the work and you get all the play, Betty number two?"

"Yes, Betty number one."

"That's not fair, is it Betty number two?"

"No it is not Betty number one. But I have no other choice. It has to be you."

"I see. I have to think about this Betty number two."

"Take your time. You want another joint?"

"Yes I do Betty number two. Go ahead and make another pot of coffee as well. I think we're going to need it."

"I'll be right back Betty number one."

Betty walks off and Betty number one stares at the exit, 'Should I or shouldn't I?'

Betty debates her decision and takes too long, for Betty number two makes it back with the pot of coffee and joints before she can make up her mind.

Betty number two pours two more cups of coffee. She hands one of them to Betty number one, along with a new joint for her to smoke.

Ten minutes later Betty number two has to know Betty number one's answer, so she asks her, "Will you help me Betty number one? If you do, you'll never have to hear me call you Betty number one again."

"And I'll never have to call you Betty number two as well I suppose?"

"Correct Betty number one."

"What can I say but yes? It's not like I can tell myself no can I?"

"You could Betty number one if you really wanted to."

"Well it's very good thing, Betty number two, that I don't want to tell you no?"

"Yes it is Betty number one."

"Well I guess there is no need in dwelling on things?"

"It's totally up to you when you want to become Eternity's Diner, Betty number one."

"That time is now Betty number two." Betty number one stands up after she puts out her joint that is nothing but a roach now. She drinks down the rest of her coffee and says to Betty number two, "Well give me a goodbye hug Betty number two."

Betty number two stands up, "It would be my pleasure to hug you Betty number one."

Betty number one walks into the room that was used by Richie and the being that was Eternity's Diner. Ten minutes later she walks back out and looks troubling at Betty number two, "I'm sorry Betty number two, I have no idea what I'm suppose to be doing in there."

"You don't?"

"No."

"But I thought if you went in there you would be granted

the same memories I did. How everything works."

"I didn't even receive a notion."

"I see... Then what now Betty number one?"

"I'm not trying to be rude but how could I possibly know this answer Betty number two?"

"I guess I was just hoping."

"I understand. So you went into that room and received all the answers Betty number two?"

"No. The being that had first control over Eternity's Diner gave them to me as he told me goodbye in my mind. If he meant to give me these answers or if it was by accident I do not know."

"There you go Betty number two. I have no way of receiving the memories you have for this being did not tell me goodbye."

"I know this but for some reason it made sense to me. Like it was going to work because it's the way things are meant to be."

"Maybe you are the one Betty number two... The only Betty to be able to run Eternity's Diner's workings."

Betty runs her hand though her hair, "I guess when you're right you're right. It's just..."

"Just what Betty?"

"If I run Eternity's Diner's workings, how am I going to leave it and spread my peace and love?"

"This I do not know either Betty the only."

Betty smiles at her older self, "Well I guess I better put you back where you belong Betty number one?"

"That would make the most sense. I cannot do anything for you, unless..."

"Unless what?"

"Unless you run Eternity's Diner and I go out and spread my peace and love."

"But that's not fair. I'm the one that is suppose to leave and have fun and excitement."

"You still will be. I am you, you are I, remember?"

"I know but still it would be you instead of me."

"That's true however before I stepped back inside Eternity's Diner I had your mind frame of how you were on June first 1969. I'm the same as you was when you first entered, if I understand this correctly."

"What are you saying Betty number one?"

"Maybe it's been me all along. You had to go through all kinds of turmoil. In you eyes I see that you are tired."

"More like hungover."

"Still, this whole ordeal has tainted you. Myself, if I weren't old I would be fresh and new to the whole idea."

"I don't know? I think you're reaching too far?"

"Let me think about this more... Did your older self that you met for the first time look as I do now?"

"Yes the very same. Why?"

"Tell me again what happened when you met your older self for the first time?"

"I walked inside here and met you. Well I met an older version of myself."

"Then what?"

"I already told you."

"Tell me again this may be very important."

"Well I also met, well I also found out that Mary and the being that ran Eternity's Diner were also present."

"Forget about them. I have a feeling that they are of no importance to what's really going on."

"Which is?"

"Finish telling me what happened and I just might be able to give you all your answers."

"I guess it's worth a try. What could it hurt?"

"Nothing that I can think of. Please continue."

"Alright. Let me see? She told me I was her younger self that she's meeting for the first time as her older self."

"And then?"

"That she was the same as I was fifty years ago when she met her older self that she has now become. I was the second half of a constant circle. She had to live fifty years to become as she is now and now it was my time to live for fifty years inside Eternity's Diner so I also could become her. The Betty you are now."

"All this heavy thinking is starting to give me a headache."

160

"Been there and still there Betty number one."

"Wait, you haven't lived fifty years inside Eternity's Diner have you Betty number two?"

"No, I haven't even lived a year inside Eternity's Diner yet."

"Interesting."

"How so?"

"You didn't follow the rules or the way your older self, Me... met your younger self, which is you of course."

"I don't understand."

"You didn't wait fifty years to become the Betty that is fifty years older. You brought me here so I could become her for you. And in doing so you would become me without the need to live fifty years inside this Eternity's Diner."

"That's... That's a mind trip Betty number one."

"Very much so."

"So how do we prove this?"

"Don't you know? Don't you know if what I said is the truth or not?"

"No I don't."

"That's a shame Betty number two. For if you don't figure this out, your dreams of peace and love through time will never exist."

"I couldn't stand that. I know I can do some good."

"I know this as well Betty number two. Try relaxing, walking around, find some calm through this storm."

"I like that Betty number one. It was very deep."

"Thank you, I try my best. If you lived fifty years longer like I have, you'd be deeper as well."

"I imagine. Wait, you didn't live fifty years longer either?"

"Haven't I?"

"No you just got here an hour or so ago."

"Time is time."

"What does that mean?"

"One hour can be an hour inside Eternity's Diner or it can become fifty years within that same hour allowed."

"So you are saying you have already became the Betty I would have become fifty years from now?"

"Yes I have. I also know a lot more than I did a few minutes ago. A whole lot more. Try thinking about everything you knew before I just asked you?"

"Okay no problem... It's gone, it's all gone. Why?"

"Because Betty number two, everything you knew now belongs to me. As it should."

"What of me? What purpose do I serve Eternity's Diner, Betty number one?"

"None Betty number two. You have already served your purpose by bringing me here to meet you. Now the circle is complete. I served my time and you served yours."

"But I didn't get my fifty years?"

"I know and who's fault is that?"

162

Betty is ashamed of herself, "It's all mine."

"Yes it is. You know what you have to do now?"

"I'm not sure Betty number one."

"Yes you do. You just said it when you said my name. I'm Betty number one, I'm the one and only Betty. All this time I thought it was all about you, when it was all about me. I'm the one who started this whole thing up by entering Eternity's Diner. You're an echo from my past that was captured and placed into my future so I could have a future created starting point that leads to the ending, I will have a hand in creating."

"What of me? Where do I go? I don't take your place outside Eternity's Diner, do I?"

"Yes you do. In a few minutes you will become who I just was before I entered my Eternity's Diner."

"Yours?"

"Yes you are now standing inside the new and improved Betty's Eternity's Diner. Do you like it?"

"No, I think it stinks. I got robbed of fifty years."

"It makes no difference Betty number two."

"Yes it does, to me anyway."

"Now it does but as soon as you exit Eternity's Diner, your memories will fade to nothing. You will look around and see no Eternity's Diner standing in front of you to enter."

"Then what Betty?"

"You will live out the rest of your life none the wiser of all that has happened."

163

"In my heart and mind I know what you're saying is the truth. I wish it was me though."

"I can understand. I get to live the next fifty years over and over again. All I have to do to repeat this for myself is do what you did and bring my discarded self back inside Eternity's Diner. I become her and she becomes me with all my memories fully intact inside her mind."

"I'm glad I could help you out."

"Help me out indeed you did. For if you didn't live your time inside Eternity's Diner like you did and lived for fifty years like I did... It would have been all about you instead of me."

"How so?"

"You would have completed the circle the way it was meant to be completed. Instead you changed things, you gave me my very own time loop I can reuse. Right before fifty years goes by all I have to do is go back to June first 1969 and pick my expelled self up before she takes off."

"You're a genius Betty."

"Thank you, I try my best."

Both Betty's have a good laugh. "Well I guess I better take off so you can start your thing up. You're not going to wait for almost fifty years before you go back to June first 1969 are you Betty?"

"No way Betty. The thought of keeping on getting this old time after time, creeps me out. No I think every ten years seems like long enough to me."

"You'll still be young enough to have a lot of fun."

"You know it and now that I'm in complete control, the fun

will never end. My life is going to be one giant party everyday."

"What about peace and love Betty?"

"That is my calling Betty and it will always be but a lady has to have a good time once in awhile. Am I right?"

"You are so very right Betty. Just don't have too good of a time or let this all go to your head. You don't want to be the one that causes everything to go wrong do you?"

"Never."

"Good, then take care Betty number one and enjoy your life or lives."

"You do the same Betty number two."

Both Betty's give the other Betty a giant goodbye hug and then Betty number two walks out of Eternity's Diner, leaving a smiling Betty the only, all to herself. The young Betty that's out of the door shakes her head to the fact that the Betty in charge is now an old lady. She shakes her head harder to her delusion. The old Betty inside Eternity's Diner talks about going back in time to this day over and over again so what can happen?

Delusion she says to herself. What happens is what just happened. The Betty that was re-invited back inside Eternity's Diner turns into the older version of Betty and takes over. While the younger version walks out the door. This makes no sense to this Betty but she's tired of the whole thing and she's glad she's getting ready to head home, where everything will be nice and normal.

Betty out the door is just about to reach her car when the sight of her hand makes her stop walking, 'No this cannot be? I've turned into the older version of Betty? That means she took my youth. What now?'

The Betty that wants her youth back turns around without a smile and with tears rolling out of her eyes. She can't believe she's been played liked this. This was suppose to be all hers and she gets nothing but an old age she didn't get the chance to live. The injustice of it all takes over her mind as she walks as fast as she can back to Eternity's Diner. Once at the doors she tries to open them but they are locked to her. She pulls and pulls but there is no give, "Betty you trickster, you deceiver... Give me back my youth, this ain't fair."

Older Betty falls to her knees with the despair of sadness engulfing her heart. With tear filled eyes she looks up at the doors, then looks into the eyes of her betrayer, "Why would you do this to me Betty?"

"I have no choice, it is the cycle of it all Betty. Your full of youth body must take over my older self as my older self takes over your younger self. I'm to be always young and free. Which makes me the light. You're always to be old and heading closer towards your grave. Which unfortunately makes you the dark."

"Then switch places with me... Let me be the one that's forever young, while you be forever old."

"No thank you Betty, I like the way things have turned out."

"You get everything."

"And why shouldn't I? This is my Eternity's Diner after all. My mission that was given to me not you. I'm more special because I came first."

"And I'm to be forever used for my youth?"

"Unfortunately yes."

"You seem similar to that of a Vampire Betty? Instead of siphoning blood from your victim, you siphon youth."

"I don't see it like this Betty. I see it more of I had to get through my darkness, you... To get to the light, myself."

"Whatever you call it Betty, you've taken from me."

"So get over it already Betty."

"How can I?"

"Accept the fact that you're playing your part in the role of my life. I need you Betty, I need your youth, this is true. I will take and take your youth from you whenever I am in need of it. In time I hope this doesn't make me feel so sad and bad."

"Oh poor you, Miss Have It All Betty. The least you can do is not whine about thorns all over your red, red roses."

"You're right Betty. Thank you for the lift up."

"Well you read my meaning wrong Betty, for I meant you no good intentions."

"Sadly I know this Betty. You are the end of the day, dark and cold. I'm the beginning of the day, bright and warm."

"You're so damn pleased with yourself, aren't you Betty?"

"You might want to take care Betty, language like that can give you wrinkles. Or more wrinkles in your case."

"Betty you younger piece of crap of myself. I would like it very much if you would stick your head inside a garbage can. Then count to three and slam the lid on top of your head as hard as you can."

"Would you now Betty? I have to say Older Betty, that was very mean and harsh of you."

"Mean? Like stealing my youth from me, younger Betty?"

167

"No matter how you feel Older Betty, your youth is mine for the taking. If you would see things in the right way, I'm sure you would understand and agree with the way things have to be."

"The only way I could ever see things like that Betty is if I were seeing it through your eyes."

"I can understand that. Well at least Betty there's one good thing that comes from out of this."

"What is that?"

"Every time I re-invite you back inside Eternity's Diner, you'll have no memory of what happens. So every time after this first time, I will not stick around for this sad part. As soon as you leave, I'm gone in time."

"How cold of you Betty. You now will close your ears to the pleas of an old woman?"

"Yes I will. It's for the best Betty. You know it is and you would do the same thing if you were in my place."

"No I would not. I would let you back in and help you. I would find anther way so that way both of us would walk away with a life worth living."

"Are you trying to lie to me, Betty? Come on be serious, we are the same person, young or old."

"So what! I'm older than you so I'm more important."

"In what world? All you can do is bake apple pies, complain and sit down. Look at me I can bend over all the way and touch my toes. You can barely think about bending over, yet alone do it."

Betty gets off her knees and wipes them off, "Why don't you go find yourself a bad trip and ride it until forever."

168

"I'll give you the last word Betty but I've got to be splitting. It's been real and all and I'll be seeing you again in ten years or so."

"How do I live my life out here like this? I can't go home?"

"That is a tough one Betty. I know what you can do, just go to an old folks home and blend in."

"The arrogance of youth. Watch out Betty that arrogance of yours might come back one day and bite you all over your pretty young ass."

"Well if it does, it better not leave any marks. Because men really like to look at my ass, especially when it's naked. It's one of my best features."

"Yes I remember, Miss High Ass."

"I think you meant to say Your Highness."

"Wait I have an idea."

"What is this idea?"

"Let me in and I'll do all the controlling of Eternity's Diner for you while you go out and have your adventures. Trust me I can and I will do this for you... For us."

"That is very nice of you Betty but if you came back inside Eternity's Diner like you are now, you would change things back to where you are the one in control and I can't, I will not have this."

"Alright then Betty. How are you going to go out on your adventures? You can't leave Eternity's Diner all by itself can you? What if someone comes strolling by and comes inside? What if they think its a good idea to take Eternity's Diner away from you? What would you do then Betty? Cry a river of regretful tears?"

169

"Not a problem Betty and thank you for caring so much."

"I don't care just tell me what you're going to do? You don't have an answer do you? Nope you're shit out of luck and you know it."

"Afraid not Betty. I'm going to use the auto pilot when I leave Eternity's Diner."

"You can't trust it, not like a real person. Things have a way of going wrong and you know it."

"Nope, I'll be fine Betty. I just know the auto pilot will work like a dream."

"Coward... At least give me a fair chance at a fight."

"No sorry I can't do that. It's starting to get late, I've got be going. And I'm sure it's time for you to be taking a nap?"

"That was so funny Betty. It would have been funnier if you would have choked while you said it."

"Wow Betty you are such an old grouch. Now you can see why I never want to become you. Yes it's for the best I'm young and pretty forever. I feel it would be much better for my complexion."

"Beauty fades Betty. If not on the outside then on the inside. You're setting yourself up for a great big fall. And when this fall happens you will be all alone with no one around to help you up."

"You're just being bitter Betty and I can't blame you for it."

"Bitter I may be Betty but at least I'm not being stupid."

"That's your twisted and harsh opinion Betty and I'll have no part of it. Goodbye older Betty, try your best to live out the rest of your life doing some good. Remember everyday great things can happen. But for this to happen you got to give it all you can."

"Before you go Betty..."

"Yes Betty?"

"You suck!"

Betty steps back, smiles and says, "Same to you Kid." Then she turns around and walks away leaving a very envious older version of herself standing there with one last hope that she'll change her mind.

Count to ten, this hope fades away as fast as Eternity's Diner does right in front of her eyes. Older Betty has one more last thing to say about things, "Well Hell."

June First 2020: A lonely figure of a man walks the streets of New York City. It is 2:22 PM and he's in no hurry. With a half smile on his face he turns down an alley and walks down it nice and calmly. Who is this man and what he has on his mind for Betty will have to wait until he's ready for it to be known. There is something though, on his wrist is a watch that's counting down from one hour and eleven minutes. Making the count down end at 3:33 PM.

It's been almost an hour since Betty the only has been inside Eternity's Diner all by herself. She's sad so she's on her second creamy and delicious, milk chocolate candy bar. In her mind keeps playing the way her older self looked like when she looked her in her eyes. Hate or very close to this was in her eyes. Betty knows she's done the right thing so she can have complete freedom to do with as she pleases.

Betty finishes her last bite as she walks around the dining room. She's starting to get bored and very much wants to now get started living her life though out time. She walks over to the counter, she picks up her almost empty

171

glass of cola and drinks it down, 'Chocolate and cola, now all I need is some grass to mellow myself out before I take my ride in time. Where, when should I go to first?'

Betty goes into the control room and orders herself a joint. She takes her time toking away and in a few minutes she's ready to get started. With excitement flowing inside her she reaches over and pulls down the lever of the auto pilot. The lights flicker then they go out through out the room. Betty breathes in deeply as the lights come fully back on. She looks around to check things out. 'Well if that's the only hitch, looks like smooth sailing from here.'

Something's wrong, Betty is expecting something to appear so she can type in commands and information for the auto pilot to follow but nothing has appeared yet, 'Okay what is going on? I know the rules, why ain't the auto pilot following them?'

Betty looks around for whatever might appear to see if it appeared someplace else around the room. She sees nothing new and she is now starting to get annoyed with how things have started for her. 'Come on Eternity's Diner, show me your stuff.'

No response. With no way of making contact with the auto pilot it leaves an annoyed Betty turning into a worried Betty. 'What am I going to do? Think, Betty think. This was not the way is was meant to be... No, not even close. I was suppose to be able to use something to give my commands to the auto pilot of Eternity's Diner. Where is it? After all I've been through, this cannot go down like this. Answers, I need some right now.' Betty tells herself.

A loud siren comes on for six straight seconds, scaring Betty out of her skin before it turns back off, 'What the Hell? I don't like this.'

A intercom sitting on a shelf turns on with a crackling noise for Betty to notice. 'This is too heavy. What is next?'

172

Coming forth from the intercom is a man's voice Betty doesn't recognize, "Hello Betty I am Auto."

"Who are you?"

"I'm Auto. In better terms, I am the auto pilot you just turned on. How can I help you Betty?"

"This is different. I wasn't expecting this... you."

"Am I bothersome to you Betty?"

"Yes to the fact, I don't know who you are."

"I am Auto..."

"Please don't tell me your Auto again. I get that your name is Auto and you're the auto pilot. But what I'd like to know is who's voice am I speaking to?"

"Betty my voice is that of the creator of Eternity's Diner."

"No it is not. I've heard his voice before, many times and it sounds nowhere even close to yours."

"Think of the voice you heard before coming forth from Eternity's Diner as a prelude to myself."

"Tell me more Auto."

"Betty think of me as an upgrade. I know what you thought you were going to receive instead of me but trust me I am a lot better. No typing, no mistakes. You talk to me, you tell me when you want to go to and I will take you there. I am here to serve you, nothing more."

"Are you now? I don't know Auto? Maybe it's me but this whole thing is starting to feel like it did when I entered Eternity's Diner for the first time? A voice on an intercom ready and willing to communicate with me. How long

173

will it be before you are the one that's giving out commands for me to follow?"

"It is not like that Betty."

"It's not Auto?"

"No Betty, it is not."

"Then how is it Auto?"

"The very same way it was before you turned me on."

'Which is?"

"You Betty, you are the one that is in charge. You give me commands and I follow them."

"That is all you do?"

"Yes... No... I can also answer questions you might have. Like is it sunny or rainy on a day you want me to take you back to or forward in time to."

"And that is all I will receive from you Auto?"

"Yes Betty."

"No big surprises later? No, I did things the wrong way now you have to take over Eternity's Diner?"

"No to that or anything even close to it Betty. Think of me simply as the mind and voice of Eternity's Diner."

"The mind I was to be Auto?"

"You still are Betty. Everything, anything you want or desire I will give it to you. You are the one in control of Eternity's Diner. I am the finite element that controls the inner workings of it."

"I like the idea of having someone... Something to talk to. But I also am feeling a little bit paranoid."

"Maybe it's that joint you smoked before you turned me on? Maybe it's simply the stress of it all?"

"Could be one of them or it could be a little bit of both."

"Do you trust me Betty?"

"I don't know Auto, it's a little too early to tell."

"Then time will be our friend Betty."

"I guess time will only tell if I can trust you or not Auto?"

"I will do my very best not to make you feel uncomfortable Betty. I will also do my very best to inform you on important information when you need it."

"I guess I cannot ask more from you than this for right now. But I will be keeping my eyes on you."

"If that is what you need to do to make yourself feel comfortable Betty, I encourage it."

"Okay before I choose when and where I want you to take me to, I have to take a pee first."

"I'll be waiting here for you Betty. I'll be waiting everywhere through out Eternity's Diner for you."

Betty pauses, "But not in the bathroom? Right Auto?"

"No everywhere but there Betty."

"Good. Now while I'm gone I want you to roll me another joint. All this stress as made my buzz go away."

"My pleasure Betty."

Chapter Six:

As Betty heads away to take her pee, within the back wall a doorway appears. When it opens up, without smoke rolling out of it, the lonely figure of a man walks through it, now boasting a larger smile. 'I'm home... The smells are still the same. This time love will prevail. This time I will be good enough for Betty to fall in love with.'

Quietly as he can Nameless Man walks out of the control room. He walks passed Betty's room, where she's in now and straight to the kitchen. There he helps himself to a slice, make that two slices of apple pie. After he sets his plate down he rubs his hands together happily and then sits down. Using his hand only, Nameless Man picks up his first piece of warm apple pie and quickly takes a big bite before its soft and flaky crust can come apart.

Buzzing sound. Nameless Man unclips his handheld from his belt. He brings it to his mouth as Betty says, "I'm back."

"Happy returns Betty."

"Yeah, it's nice to be back. You're not going to ask me about my time in the bathroom, are you Auto?"

"No and I do not care to Betty. Chill out and smoke your joint. Let me talk your ears off as you kick back and relax."

"Sounds good to me. It's been a very long day so far and I could use a buzzing break to calm my mind and being."

"You make it sound so nice Betty."

"Auto if we are to become Friends in the future, I would like to become them without you kissing my ass in the process."

"Excuse me?"

"You heard me Auto. Don't try so hard. Let your true self shine out more brightly."

"I can do that Betty. How much of my true self would you like me to be?"

"As much as you can be. Well as much as you can be without you becoming dangerous."

"I'm not dangerous Betty."

"I surely hope not. This movie doesn't need a horror scene popping out and changing things so that way the story line can become darker."

"Betty I'm more like a beach scene, where we sit down in the sand, drink wine and enjoy each other's company. No dark and rainy skies, just beautiful blue skies with great, big, white clouds."

"Wine?"

"Why not?"

"Aren't you part of the machine?"

"...Yes."

"Well shouldn't you be wanting to drink.... Oh I don't know? Maybe oil?"

"...Oil's not on the menu Betty."

"You sound hurt Auto? Did I hurt your mechanical feelings?"

"Not at all Betty. I'm above that."

"Are you now? I wonder?"

"There is nothing for you to wonder Betty. I am what I am and this can never change."

"No wizard behind the curtain?"

Nameless Man takes the last bite of his second slice of apple pie and places it slowly inside his mouth. He sits back and shakes his head to the delight that is Betty. He knows he's paused enough and needs to give his answer to her, "No Betty I'm not behind the curtain. I'm in the kitchen just getting through eating apple pie."

Betty chokes out her big hit of weed and then coughs out strongly. After she's calmed down, with a burning chest and watery eyes, she simply says, "What?" And then she stands up slowly. She takes a few steps forward and asks, "Are you really in the kitchen?"

Nameless Man, thinks quickly, "That's funny Betty."

"Why is that Auto?"

"You believed my joking around with you as if it is the truth. Come now Betty, you're better than this."

Betty straightens up, "Yes I am."

"You told me to be more of my true self."

"Yes I did but..."

"I like to have fun. The only way I can have any fun at all is when I'm talking to you. I was happy when you told me I could be more of myself. If this is a problem, I can change the way I talk to you without any personality at all? I will become more machine like, so cold and without feelings. But I'd be glad to become this for you Betty, if you need, if you want me to?"

Betty looks at the intercom, feeling bad inside, "No Auto.

No Auto, I would not like you nor would I like anyone to become like that. If what you said about being in the kitchen eating apple pie was a joke, it was funny. I would have laughed if I knew you were joking around."

"I didn't say I was eating apple pie Betty. I said I just got through eating apple pie."

Betty laughs and Auto follows suit, "You're a riot Auto. Maybe we have a chance at making this work."

"If not, it will not be because of my fault."

"Jokingly you mean that I will be the one to be at fault?"

"Correct."

"Damn, can't a hippy lady get a break?"

"Not today. And why would you think that you deserve one anyway?"

"Because Auto, I have a very sweet smile."

"This is true."

"Thank you."

"Not a problem. Would you like another joint or something to drink Betty?"

"I'm good on the joint front but I'm getting thirsty so I'll take a beer or two."

"That's my Betty. Here's two cold ones ready to go."

"About time. What took you so long?" Betty responds back as two bottles of beer appear instantly in front of her.

"Is that a joke Betty?"

Betty opens up her beer and takes two drinks from it, "Nope Auto, I was being as serious as I can be. Next time you take this long, I'm throwing you into the garbage can."

"That's funny Betty. Why don't you throw that joke you just said in it first? So that way I won't be lonely."

"We're going to have some great times together Auto. I can just feel it."

"As I do Betty."

Betty drinks down her beer, "Wow I have to pee again. I'll be right back. Don't go away."

"How can I Betty?" Auto asks jokingly.

Betty walks slowly out of the door of the control room and than slowly to her bedroom. When she reaches it, instead of entering it she runs as fast as she can to the kitchen. Once there she burst through the doors panting and sees? Taken aback all Betty can do is ask, "Who are you?"

"You are such a trickster Betty. I trusted you."

"Who are you to trust me Stranger? Shouldn't it be about me trusting you?"

"Yes."

"So you're the face that belongs to the voice I've been talking with?"

"Yes I am."

"Where did you come from?"

"It's more like when."

"When then Auto? If that's your real name?"

180

"No my real name is not Auto. I just picked that name for obvious reasons."

"Goody gum drops. What is your real name Stranger?"

"Eric, my real name is Eric."

"Alright Eric, now that we got out of the way, what do you want?"

"Well Betty, since everything is messed up, my only answer can be is you."

"Me? You want me? Why?"

"I'd rather not explain."

"Tough peaches. If you want me not to freak out and start throwing things at you, you better give me information."

"Okay... One day, a long, long time from now, four people together created a time machine."

"Four? I thought you created it by yourself?"

"No it was the four of us."

"Four of us?"

"Yes, you and I and Mary and Richie."

"You've got to be kidding me? Do you think I would believe a story like that Eric?"

"It's not a story Betty."

"Wait? Eric? Mary's Eric?"

"Yes and no. True I was Mary's husband but my heart always has belonged to you."

"How could it? I don't even know anything about you besides your name is Eric."

"Yes you do, you just don't remember."

"If your heart belongs to me then I must assume my heart belonged to you?"

"That is very true, we were in love. Very much so."

"If this is true then why did you marry Mary?"

"It was the way things worked out."

"Why? How come?"

"I... Mary and I ended up together and you and Richie ended up together."

"Huh? Make sense Eric."

"We, you and I were a couple. Them, Mary and Richie were a couple when we created the time machine we dubbed Eternity's Diner."

"How nice Eric, but I'm still not getting the big picture."

"The four of us are friends. We were friends before we became couples. We all worked together at Mitford's."

"Mitford's? Never heard of it."

"Maybe if things go right this time, you will remember that you worked there. Maybe you might even remember everything, including us."

"I guess it would be nice to be let out of the darkness."

"I've tried so many times to makes this happen for you. To get us back together mentally but..."

"But what?"

"You Betty... For some reason you are the only one of us that has never remembered what truly happened."

"Why is this Eric?"

"I don't know and it's been driving me crazy."

"So both Richie and Mary remembered creating Eternity's Diner together? The four of us creating it?"

"Yes they have. They've been making things very hard on me. Very hard for me to get to this point."

"I don't understand."

"They want out."

"Out of what?"

"Out of Eternity's Diner."

"How come?"

"Because mentally the four of us have been inside Eternity's Diner for years and years. The both of them want out and they're getting close to the point that they might be willing do anything they have to do to make this happen."

"This sounds dangerous?"

"It is and it could be a lot worse if it weren't for you Betty."

"Me? Why me Eric?"

"Because you are special."

"Don't give me that routine Eric. Give it to me straight."

"Alright Betty I will but if you don't mind I would like to do some things first?"

"Like what Eric?"

"Well I would like to take a piss. Then I would like to drink a beer, while smoking a joint."

"That can be arranged Eric."

"Yes I know Betty, I'm the one that makes thing happen inside Eternity's Diner."

"We need to talk about that as well."

"Betty I have to know, do you like me a little bit?"

"Yes you're nice to look at and I also like your voice. It calms me. But of course we're talking only about a bit of like towards you."

"That's good enough for a start."

"And it just might remain there. Us being a we in another life time outside Eternity's Diner is something I have to ponder. I'm going to have to watch you very closely at first. Make sure you're up to muster."

"That's fine with me. Test my knowledge. I will give it to you straight, while I'm telling you the truth."

"I like this very much Eric."

"Betty there might be a faster way to get your memory back. One we've never tried but I've asked you many times to try..."

"And?"

"And you've always said no."

"And why would I say no to you about this every time? Is it maybe that it's dangerous?"

"No it's not dangerous at all."

"Then tell me. I just might say yes this time."

"Maybe later after we get to know each other better."

"Shouldn't it be getting to know you? You know me already. What? Have I changed?"

"Yes many times over. I personally like this young hippy lady version of yourself that you created this time for yourself."

"Really? I created this version of myself?'

Eric laughs a little, "Naw, I'm just messing with you."

"Why would you do this to me Eric? I'm all confused, I'm grasping for any kind of hint of a memory."

"I... You've always had a great sense of humor. In fact so do I. It's one of the things we like most about the other. Well this and our bodies. Preferably naked bodies."

"Naked bodies? Sounds great. I've haven't had body contact with another human in awhile."

"Really? I can't believe it. Making love was the thing I've been wanting to try and you've always said no to."

"Did you always ask me first?"

"I don't? Yes I did."

"There you go. It just had to come down to me saying yes without you asking me first."

"That must have been it alright. I'm so glad."

"Well you can still be glad, even gladder after you get back from taking your piss."

"When you're right Betty, you're right."

Eric walks off and Betty keeps her eyes on him, 'I just knew it when I first laid eyes on him it would come down to sex. It's not like I don't want to. It's just like I shouldn't. Besides how do I know he's telling me the truth? For all I know he can be a hitchhiker looking for a good time? Still I don't know? The way he looks at me is like the way I'm looked at when a guy likes me. In Eric's case, really likes me. What should I do? I don't fear him so I'm going to let this play out for awhile longer. I want to get to the truth.'

Eric walks back from out of the control room where he took his piss and Betty is sitting at the counter waiting for him. They have some small talk while they drink three beers a piece, while sharing two joints. They both feel nice and relaxed so Betty decides it's time for some more answers. "Eric let's get back to me, you, Mary and Richie. About the way we created Eternity's Diner together."

"My pleasure Betty. The four of us worked so hard. Separately, not one of us would have came even close to creating the majesty that's Eternity Diner. It was like it was meant to be when the four of us got together."

"Like magic Eric?"

"More like fate Betty."

"Please go on Eric. You've got me very curious."

"The four of us created Eternity's Diner together. When it was completed, the four of us entered it together as one united team of friends and lovers. Then something went wrong. Really wrong."

"What went wrong Eric?"

"The four of us got separated in time. Before I got comfortable, I got expelled from Eternity's Diner. Luckily the fail safe we added worked and I was expelled out on June first 2020."

"Why June first 2020? Is that the same day we entered Eternity's Diner together?"

"Not even close Betty. We picked that day, well because we had to pick a day for the fail safe. I think it was you? Yes Betty it was you that chose June first 2020."

"I wonder why?"

"I don't know."

"Maybe I'll remember later."

"There's always the chance Betty."

"True Eric, go on please."

"I had the fail safe to use and when I used it I did my best to find the three of you. It was unreal. None of you took me serious when I found you. The three of you somehow inserted yourselves in time as people that had real, reality lives to live and die with. A few times it was all I could do to barely save your lives."

"Seriously Eric?"

"Seriously Betty. You can't account for the many variables I had to contend with. A car out of nowhere trying it's best to run you over. Burning buildings. Heck I even saved Richie once from a plane crash."

"Sounds dreadful and horrible Eric?"

"Sometimes Betty, but not all the time. Sometimes we even had a great time."

"That's nice to know."

"I would save one of the three of you and before I could expel you out of Eternity's Diner on June first 2020, you would slip back or forward through time. Then I had to try and find you again only to have every one of you slip back in time."

"Even when it was nice, you still had to save one of us every time Eric?"

"No not all. A lot of times after I had one of you believing me about Eternity's Diner and time traveling, you would slip in time away from me just like after I saved you."

"That is very strange."

"It took me years of trying and trying to finally get somewhat of a hold on the situation. I created the time loop the three of you could only use from June first 1919 to June first 2018."

"And it worked?"

"Not all the way, I still had a lot of problems to handle. But by creating this time loop it made things a whole lot easier on me."

"After this Eric, what happened?"

"Richie and Mary had their awakening as I like to call it."

"Awakening Eric?"

"Yes Betty, their awakening."

"I didn't have one?"

"No Betty and you still haven't had one."

"I wonder why just me? Why didn't I have my awakening?"

"I have no answer for you Betty."

"Then what Eric?"

"By having their awakening it meant Richie and Mary knew what was happening every time I found them."

"But not me Eric?"

"No Betty, sorry."

"Did Mary and Richie try to help you?"

"Yes but every time something happened and they went back or forward through time before I could expel them. After countless times the both of them had enough and wanted me to let you die in time."

"They did? Why?"

"They thought, they hoped, your death would reset things back to the start."

"Did you believe this Eric?"

"No I didn't Betty."

"Good."

"Yes very good Betty. For after awhile both Richie and Mary got stronger. They got more of a hold to make things happen to you. I saved your life more than a few times from their failed attempts on your life."

"Thank you Eric. I can't believe Mary and Richie would do this to me."

189

"They're scared Betty. They're afraid that some how, some way fate will use its power and place the both of them in time where they can't try to make anymore changes to it."

"Do you believe this Eric?"

"I don't know what I believe anymore Betty. I've lived through so very much."

"I can understand. What you remember living through over and over, sounds so exhausting."

"But in the end it's all about you Betty. And to me your worth every minute I have to spend back or forward in time. I will get you out of Eternity's Diner, I promise you."

"Maybe Eric I don't really want to leave? Or maybe I can't, or I'm not allowed to leave?"

"Perhaps Betty, anything is possible."

"So Richie and Mary are still after me?"

"Yes. They are waiting for me to fail again so they can have their try at you again."

"Well here's to hoping you don't fail me this time Eric."

"Yes indeed. To make their chances harder on them, I made some very hard decisions."

"Like what Eric?"

"I paired the four of us up. So that way you would be a little safer."

"Did it work?"

"Almost. There was a flaw in the design."

"Like how so?"

"It was suppose to be you and I that got paired up and Richie and Mary that got paired up."

"That's not what happened though?"

"I know you know the answer to this Betty?"

"Yes. Richie and I got paired up and you and Mary got paired up."

"Yes no matter what I've tried I cannot change this. It's almost like fate wants it this way."

"Maybe it does Eric. I have questions?"

"Ask away Betty."

"You and Mary, you both know what's going on every time things get reset?"

"Yes."

"So the two of you live together as a married couple? Doing what?"

"Doing what married couples do."

"Until what?"

"Until Mary makes me choke to death on her delicious apple pie. Then she waits for us to stop by and pick her up in 1973."

"Why would we have to pick her up?"

"It's the way it has to play out. And her apple Pie."

"More information please."

"Mary has to make her appearance in the story. Richie and you are already have roles in."

"Then what?"

"The four of us are together waiting on you to remember so that way we can make our way out of Eternity's Diner."

"What about Richie and I? Why ain't we a couple like you and Mary?"

"Because of you. You get it on a few times with Richie and that's all you want from him. After that it's just good friends between the two of you."

"When do they try to hurt me? Is that coming next?"

"No, that time has passed."

"They didn't try to hurt me this time?"

"No, they thought, they hoped tricking you out of Eternity's Diner would make you so mad and sad at the same time that it would shock you into remembering."

"So their chance at tricking me more or hurting me is over with for this version of the continuing story of Betty's Eternity's Diner."

"Yes it is."

"What's next?"

"You always fade away back to June first 1969."

"So this is the final act of the story?"

"Yes it is."

"So what, we make love and I remember?"

192

"I'd like to believe this."

"What if I don't?"

"Then I would have made love one last time with the love of my life."

"What if it does work? What if I remember? Then what do we do, discontinue Eternity's Diner?"

"Yes."

"I have a feeling this is why I always go back to June first 1969. I like Eternity's Diner, I like what I've been through. The struggle to have complete control over it as the three of you do your best to take it away from me."

"It has to be done Betty. The three of us want our lives back. So should you. I'm afraid to move, I don't want to start over again. The way you are this time, I think we can have success."

"The four of us back in the time when we belong in?"

"Yes, you'll love it. It's like nothing you've lived through in Eternity's Diner can compare to. In our time life is so easy. All over the world free food, water and shelter."

"So there is no struggle? Nobody wants for nothing for everything they need is provided for them?"

"Exactly Betty. I'm so glad you've stayed here for this long this time. All it takes is one of us to change the way the story line is, too much and you fade away back to June first 1969. We were hoping when Richie and Mary took away Eternity's Diner that you wouldn't repeat this if you didn't get your memory back."

"Why don't I remember what is truly going on when I go back to June first 1969?"

"That's because of the three of us. We can't take the chance you'll take over and expel the three of us back to our time and stay within Eternity's Diner and make changes. Changes that can change the future. Perhaps changing things to where we do not exist."

"The four of us can make this whole thing stop. No more Betty's Eternity's Diner?"

"Yes we can. Now if you'll just stay calm and relaxed Betty, I can let Richie and Mary join us. They would be very glad to see you this way."

"Everything's a lie Eric?"

"What Betty?"

"There's no Betty 1969. Did I or you really create her? Is Betty even my name in the real world?"

"You are the one that created Betty. You are the one that created all our lives within Eternity's Diner. You are the one in control and the only way we can stop you from having complete control is by making you lose your memory every time you head back to June first 1969. And no your name is not Betty and mine is not Eric and the same goes for Richie and Mary."

"All this is because of me?"

"When the four of us entered Eternity's Diner we messed up things. We made a few little mistakes that change the way history unfolded. In time we corrected these mistakes and then the four of us agreed to leave Eternity's Diner and dismantle it. You lied Betty, you betrayed us. You created these lives for us so you wouldn't be alone."

"This cannot be true? I wouldn't do these things. I'm a good person that wants to spread peace and love."

"No that is Betty. In real life you are nothing like this. You are our team leader, we are your crew. Something in your mind likes this Betty you created so much you've been trying to find a way to become her permanently."

"While leaving the three of you out in the cold, so to say? You do not want to live inside Eternity's Diner and you cannot allow me to stay inside it without you?"

"Yes. Please Betty set things back to the way things should be. Give us our lives back."

"Why do you still call me Betty?"

"Because that is one big no. If we call you by your real name or call ourselves by our real names you fade back to June first 1969. Will you allow Richie and Mary to join us?"

"Yes. It would be nice to see them again with my full memory almost intact. But first, one more thing?"

"You got it."

"Making love. Were you serious or were you just playing along with the story line?"

"I was just playing along with the story line. The big climax that never happens."

"You sound bitter Eric?"

"So many times we've been this close to making love then you fade away leaving me so wanting you. This is the first time we've gone past talking about or almost making love."

"I know Eric. Bring in Richie and Mary."

"You know? You've gotten your memory back Betty?"

"Yes Eric, it was all about avoiding the forbidden kiss. Or

195

forbidden making love in our case. If I would have made love with you, you would have taken over. Well Richie and Mary would've been doing their handy work while you avoided my attention. My memory would have come back to me and the four of us would then exit Eternity's Diner without time for cuddling between us."

"That is a harsh way of saying it. We've made love many times together Betty before we entered Eternity's Diner."

"I remember and I enjoyed every time for I love you Eric."

"I love you Betty and I've missed you."

"But I'm sure Mary satisfied you in my absence?"

"That was not my fault. You made this happen between Mary and I."

"I know Eric. I guess deep inside I felt bad for abandoning you, so I gave you Mary for comfort."

"Maybe so Betty. We had a some good times but I think it was more out of boredom and frustration."

Mary and Richie walk through the doors of Eternity's Diner, full of excitement. Mary speaks first, "Well what's going on Eric? Betty?"

Richie has to let it be known that he's there as well, "Yeah what's going on?"

Eric answers them, "My friends Betty remembers what is going on. We will finally be able to leave Eternity's Diner."

"Did the two of you make love? Is this what made the difference? If it is, it didn't take you long. Poor Betty."

"No Mary we didn't make love for if we did we would still be making love for Betty satisfies me," Eric tells her loudly.

"Then why does Betty know what's going on?" Richie asks Eric, sounding like he's running out of patience.

"Why don't you ask her?"

"There is no need Richie, I will be glad to tell you and also tell you Mary. I just had to get passed the point where Eric and I were going to make love. After this didn't happen bingo my memories back."

"Good now let's go home." Mary demands.

"Yes my friends let's go home. I have to apologize to the three of you. It was very selfish of me to make you live out your lives back in time. I had the advantage of not remembering. You three, how many times did I make you relive this over and over again?"

"Way too many times Betty," Mary assures her.

"Before I release control, would any of the three of you like one last look around?"

All three answer, "No." at the same time.

"Very well, let's go home. But first I have to know. Do the three of you forgive me?"

All three answer, "Yes." at the same time.

"Thank you my friends. I couldn't ask for better and more understanding friends. In our time there is no need for want, everything is provided for us. The chance to live a life where things are so different from our time was just too tantalizing to me. I wanted adventures, where I met people from the past and tried my best to understand their lives and the way they lived them."

"But that want and desire is over with? Right Betty?" Eric asks questioningly.

197

"Yes it is and happily so I might add. Now that I have my thoughts back I wonder why I did this in the first place."

"You sounds so much like the way you truly are Betty," Eric informs her.

"I'm back Baby."

"I don't want to seem uncaring to the two of you but I want out of here. I can barely contain my excitement."

"Yes same for me. I really need to get out of here before I jump out of my skin," Richie adds.

"Relax my friends we'll be out of here in a few moments."

Betty adjust herself and the control she's had over everything and everyone is now over with. Four friends hug and laugh as they walk towards the real exit of Eternity's Diner. At the last moment Betty pulls away from the embrace of her friends and says, "I forgot something."

The timing for Betty doing this was passed the time allowed for her three friends to wait for her before they were forced to make their way to the already closing door provided for them. Once back out three friends all together turn back around to see the doorway close up. Eric runs towards nothing yelling, "No Betty, come back."

Mary gives Eric a moment of silence before she tells him, "We tried our best. There is nothing we can do now. Betty is now lost in time."

Richie has to add, "There must be something we can try?"

Eric rubs his hand on his head, "I know this doesn't make a difference now but for Betty I want us to remain calling ourselves the names she created for us inside Eternity's Diner. Only until we try to find her?"

"That is fine with me Eric. We at least owe Betty this for getting us out of Eternity's Diner," Mary tells him calmly.

"Yes let's do this for Betty," Richie agrees.

Eric fools with controls trying to find out where Betty is so that he can go back into Eternity's Diner and bring her back. He checks and checks and finds no trace of her, "This cannot be? Nothing. There is no trace of her back in time. I cannot find Betty."

"What does that mean Eric?" Mary asks nervously.

"I don't know Mary. I just don't know. As far as I can tell Betty does not exist back in time. It's like she's been erased from time."

"You mean she's dead Eric?" Richie asks sadly.

"In a sense yes Richie but it's more like she never existed at all."

"How can this be Eric? Betty was born after this?"

"I guess time reset itself. This is the only answer I can think of Mary. What a way to go, to never exist."

"If Betty never existed Eric, then why do we remember her so well?"

"Because Richie, Eternity's Diner still exists."

"What happens after we dismantle it Eric?"

"We'll probably forget Betty ever existed as well."

"If you don't want to dismantle Eternity's Diner Eric, Mary and I will understand."

"Thank you Richie but I know, as well as the two of you

know, that Eternity's Diner is too dangerous to let remain standing. Betty or not we can't risk anything happening back in time again. I guess this is our price for tempting the hands of fate."

Mary and Richie say nothing as they pull up their sleeves to help their very, sad friend do something he doesn't want to do. Before they can get started, with tears in their eyes Eternity's Diner disappears without a trace.

Three people look around their surroundings and at the other two people they are with and wonder what is going on. They have no thoughts of Betty, Eternity's Diner or what they are doing here. They nervously talk among themselves finding out nothing. After twenty seven minutes of not knowing what is going on three strangers say goodbye to each other. They walk away and never see the other again for the rest of their lives.

Epilogue

It has been one year since Maria, now forever known as Betty, made her escape and erased herself from history. In the short time it took her friends to discover she was erased from time, Betty was setting things up so she can create Eternity's Diner before she and her friends did the first time around. What took about a month for Betty to set things up perfectly for Eternity's Diner this time around, only took minutes for her friends to be crying over her loss to not remembering her or remembering each other.

Things are very different in this final version of Betty's Eternity's Diner. There is never conflict inside, for there is no one besides Betty that resides within it. With deep thought she rearranged the auto pilot so it was truly part of the machine.

She gave it a man's voice she liked to hear and this is the only thing humanlike she allowed it to obtain. For she knows she can be the only human element in the equation or it will collapse around itself. Time is fickle as Betty rides the fine lines of it back and forth without causing any harmful out stretching waves.

Thus Ends Betty Eternity's Diner. It is 2:17 PM on April 2nd 2018. I almost ended this book as if the whole story was nothing but a dream. I liked what I had in mind for when Betty woke up from this Odyssey dream but in the end I put this dream ending to rest and went on. I feel I made the best decision so Betty's story can continue forth.

It was a lot of fun taking the short dark version of Eternity's Diner and turning it and switching it around until it became what lies before this. You can be sad for Betty or you can appreciate the wisdom of her victory.

For appreciation for buying this book I am including a extra short Betty story for you. All you have to do is turn the page to find out what kind of adventure or misadventure Betty is getting ready to have. Enjoy.

Keith Starblue

Betty Helps Misty Find Her Missing Ring
(Pages 202-216)

It's a nice and gentle seventeenth of September 1985 for thirty years old Misty Rogers of Plate, Utah. She is so very sad, she's tired of crying tears of sadness and anger. Somewhere, somehow she lost her Mother's wedding ring. A ring she's been wanting to put on her finger for years. She can't believe that now, when she has the chance to get married to a great man like Wayne, she has lost it.

On her deathbed ten years ago her mother Berenice took this ring off her finger and handed it to her and told her to find a love that is as true as hers and her father's was. Ten minutes later with this ring in a death grip in her right hand, Misty the sole survivor of her family, watched her mother pass away painfully then calmly at the very end.

Years of trying to find Mister Right has broken her spirits. Four years ago she decided to limit her expectations and decided a man that keeps coming back for more was better than no man at all. Last year she got tired of dirt bags, as Misty likes to refer to them, and in the process she decided to give up on finding love.

Love has a way of finding you when you want it or are looking for it. It also has a way of finding you if you're not looking for it or even want it. Misty slows down her crying and remembers how she met Wayne.

Six months ago, Misty with no smile of happiness on her lips and in her eyes, but dressed to make a man beg and pant, walked into a bar she hadn't been to in years. Once she entered, all eyes were on her. She drew off this attention and added it to her strut as she walked by men that wanted to get to know her instantly.

A few grabs and smacks later, Misty found herself at the bar. She sat down and the man that sat next to her, that she hadn't even pay attention to said to her,

"Thanks but no thanks. I'd rather be alone tonight."

Misty, taken back by this, was about to give it to him when he turned to face her and looked into the eyes of the most beautiful woman he'd ever seen. Misty waited five seconds then calmly asked him, "Why don't you take a picture?"

He smiled deeply at her and responded back with, "I'd rather have a painting of you that way I could hang it on my wall and stare at it everyday."

Misty smiled and laughed a little. She tried to fight back that old feeling of unbridled lust, she liked so very much but refused to be partnered with anymore. She's better than this and she reminded herself as she started to cool down on the inside. "Rather than have you worshiping me tonight, I'd rather you just donate a few drinks to the lady that is the idol of your future, very wet dreams."

"Do you want to know my name before I start dreaming about you?"

Misty is in a good mood and wants to have some fun, "No, not really."

"Well my name is Mars."

"Mars? Mars what?"

"Just Mars."

"Are you famous?"

"Only when I'm naked."

Misty liked this so she gave Mars the three second kiss of I like you so don't mess things up. "You're welcome Mars."

"Thank you?"

"Mis... Venus, with no last name as well."

"I thought you looked familiar. It's great to see you again Venus. How's Saturn?"

"How should I know? I dropped that over expressive planet eons ago."

"Good for you, you never needed him. So that means I finally get my chance? After waiting so many centuries, I finally get my chance to look upon splendor?"

"Damn Mars, you're pushing all the right buttons. So what's up with what you said to me when I first sat down beside you?"

"I'm down on love. Who needs it, was in my mind until I looked into your eyes."

"Thank you Mars, that is very sweet."

"Sweet enough for another kiss?"

"Why not? My lips are not too busy to enjoy some nice, random kissing right now."

"I really dig you Venus. You're one of a kind."

"Remember this and you might just win my heart."

"I would love to offer you my heart before I win yours."

"That is the noble thing to do Mars."

"I try Venus."

"Well come to me and receive your kiss."

"Can I use my tongue?"

"I tell you what Mars, if I like your tongue then I'll use mine as well."

"If you don't like my tongue Venus?"

"Then I'll have to bite it off. Sorry this is not my rule. Blame the universe buddy, if you have any problems with the outcome you don't desire to experience."

"I'll be glad to take my chances Venus. If my worth is not mighty, then I do not deserve your love."

"Love?"

"Okay... Your body for the night."

"That's more like it... Wait I want love not lust."

"Why would you want this Venus? Love betrays, while lust gives you the same unloving feelings every time."

Misty looks deeply into a man's, a stranger's eyes and wishes that they would fall in love tonight. "Take your kiss Mars before your chance leaves without a trace. By the way my name is Misty."

"My name is Wayne." Two lonely people that gave up on love got turned on.

This second kiss lasted long enough for people to take notice, including an old lover of Misty's that she had dropped to the wayside two years ago. He watched her and wanted her until surprisingly his date asked him, "Do you know her?"

He quickly turned to save himself by saying, "Know who?"

"That lady... Well that sex object over there?"

"No I've never seen her before. I was just thinking..."

"Thinking what?" His now angry dates demanded.

"How much luckier I would be if that was me and you kissing like that."

"Why's that?"

"Because you are so much prettier than she is."

And old discarded lover of another lover gets a very big surprise as his date gave him a kiss to match the two lovers she was just complaining about. Right after their lips stopped touching and they pulled away to look each other in the eye, Misty and Wayne walked by. Misty said, "Hey Billy, I haven't seen you since I broke up with your cheating ass a few years ago. How have you been?"

Misty pulled on Wayne's hand and they walked away together before a shattered Billy could answer her back. "I thought you told me you didn't know her Billy?"

Billy, who was all nervous and wanted things to go back to the way they were a few heartbeats ago, didn't wait to think so he said, "Misty let me explain."

"Misty? Is that her name? Billy did you just really call me by her name?"

"I'm sorry, I didn't..."

"Matters not to me cheater. I'm glad that slut came by and set me straight before I made a mistake again." Jane stood up, she took a sip from her full drink and then she poured the rest on Billy's crotch. "Thanks for such a great time Billy. It will be hard pressed for another man to top you this night." Jane walked away feeling mad and happy.

Misty made Wayne stop at the doorway so she could see the outcome of her passing by handy work on Billy. She laughed as she watched the decent looking lady he was kissing pour her drink all over his crotch. Embarrassed Billy looked around and made eye contact with Misty. She flicked him off then she pulled Wayne out the door.

Once out and five steps away from the doors, Wayne slowed down and asked Misty, "Damn Misty why did you bust that man's balls so bad?"

Misty stopped walking and looked Wayne in his eyes and said, "Because he deserved it. I gave him my heart and he cheated on me."

"I understand."

"You better."

"Wow take a step back Misty. Don't be angry with me just because I'm a man. Yes I am a man but I am not that man. I am very proud to tell you that I am my very own man that never claims the mistakes of other men."

"How righteous of you."

"Thank you I try my very best. Shall we continue on Misty, or is this great moment going to fade away to dust?"

"No dust Wayne just lust. Come on take me home."

"I can't, I don't have a home. I live in my car. You looking for a roommate Misty?"

Misty stopped walking once again and looked at Wayne like she couldn't believe what he just said to her, "Are you serious Wayne? Or are you messing with me?"

"Guilty of messing with you, Misty."

"Did you have fun?"

"Very much. How about you?"

"Not so much and now I'm bored so I'm going home alone. You are a very dumb man Wayne. You know this?"

"I used to know this but I forgot all about it so many years ago. So now it's like it never really existed in the first place."

"What an answer Mars."

"Wayne, Baby."

"Baby? Wayne, baby is something you would have called me while you were making love to me."

"So I don't get to make love to you now?"

"Nope."

"Well that sucks. Well can you at least buy me a really expensive dinner?"

"Why would I do that?"

"Because I'm not hungry. Well not for food."

"Do you have a place? Is it nice? Does it have a bed? Or do we have to do it on the floor?"

"Let me see... Yes. Yes. Yes. And only if you want to?"

"I want to have a great time tonight Wayne. So no broken promises. No I love you's. If this becomes something more than for one night. Let's just let it flow. I don't want to rush. I don't want to give myself one more time to a man that uses me until he's had enough."

"I get that, I've lived that. I'd like to once find a lady that likes to stay home and just make love all night instead of going out with friends. We meet, we like the other, we get hot. Then they're happy to have someone in their life they start to spend less time with after the excitement of new love starts to wear off. Count to ten and it's over with. Why does this happen, you ask Misty?"

"I sure do Wayne."

"I think it's a fear of pulling too far away from the herd."

"I think you're damn on the spot Wayne. So you win seven minutes of time you can use towards making love to me."

"I've barely gotten started in seven minutes Misty. Can you spot me an hour to add to my seven minutes?"

"One hour and seven minutes?"

"You can longer if you want Misty."

"That's very manly of you Wayne but alas I think we'll just stick with seven minutes only."

"Well sexy that is such a shame so instead of making love to you, I'll just kiss you for seven minutes."

"Really? You'd give up making love to me just to kiss me?"

"In a heartbeat Misty. You're a very pretty, built lady."

"Yeah I know. I've really kept my figure, haven't I?"

"Yes you have."

"Wayne are you telling me I look good for my age?"

"Hell no Misty."

"Good."

After this Wayne drove Misty to his place leaving her car behind at the bar to be picked up later tonight or tomorrow morning. As soon as Misty entered Wayne's place she felt at home. To her mind it was like this would be her place if she were him. Wayne showed her his place as Misty discovered he was a lot like her. Both of them are alone in this world with friends but no family to call their own. Both of them are givers and wishers. Both of them have been heartbroken more than one human being should be heartbroken.

A few shots drank down and Misty told Wayne to take her to his bedroom. Together they stayed there until they fell asleep in each other's arms. When they woke up, they both wanted to make love again but both of them decided it would be better if they waited until after they both brushed their teeth, for both of them had death breath.

The next morning talk was fast as both agreed that they would like to see the other again later that night. Only this time they were to meet up at Misty's place. Days turned into weeks. Weeks turned into months as both lovers, love the other more. Last month, five months since they've been dating Wayne asked Misty to marry him. With bent knee he handed her his ring. She said yes before he slid her ring on her finger.

Misty was so happy when Wayne said yes to using her parent's wedding rings. Misty's mother Berenice wore her dead husband's, Paul's wedding ring around her neck on a gold necklace. Misty was willed this officially along with her mother's wedding ring. She was also willed her family's home and her mother's car. She sold them both. She had no need for a second car and the house she grew up in felt too big for her when she stayed in it all alone.

The past slips away from Misty's mind as the present comes back fully to her. Wayne's ring is there but hers is missing. More tears run down her cheeks as she wonders what she's going to do. Her tummy rumbles so she decides to treat herself to a hamburger and fries. Out the door and into her car, she drives to town.

Half way there Misty slows down because she sees something she's never seen before on this road. A diner out of nowhere, 'What is going on? This diner wasn't here before?'

Misty feels like eating someplace new so she slows down even more and then she pulls into this diner's empty parking lot. She stops her car and turns it off. Misty then looks out her windshield and reads the glowing sign, 'Eternity's Diner,' she says to herself out loud.

Misty shakes her head at the name of this Diner. She gets out of her car and smells apple pie instantly. This causes her tummy to rumble even more louder, 'Wow that smells so good. I think I'll have a slice of this amazing smelling apple pie along with my burger and fries.'

Misty walks to the doors of Eternity's Diner and enters them. Inside she hears a song she's never heard before playing on this futuristic looking jukebox. She looks passed the jukebox and towards the counter and sees Betty, who's smiling at her. "Hello welcome to Eternity's Diner. I am Betty, the owner of this one of a kind Diner."

A little taken back Misty answers back with a simple, "Hello Betty, I'm Misty."

"Have a seat Misty and let me know what I can create for you today?"

"Create? I never heard of it that way before but oh well it's not going to stop me."

"Good. What would you like Misty?"

Still standing in front of the counter Misty places her order. "I would like a burger with fries, a piece of apple pie, a glass of ice water and a frosty cold beer."

"Would you like your burger with everything?"

"Yes I would."

"Would you like it deluxe with bacon and cheese?"

"How much extra will that be?"

"Don't worry about it Misty, it's on me."

"Oh no Betty, I know how little money... You own this Diner? Yes you do. Thank you Betty this is very nice of you especially since you have no other customers inside your Diner besides me."

"Don't let it bother you Misty, believe me I do not. Eternity's Diner is something special I created. Please have a seat and I'll show you just how special it truly is."

Misty looks at Betty with intrigue in her eyes then she sits down and says, "Show me what you got Betty."

"My pleasure Misty. Now look down in front of you."

Misty does as Betty asks of her and in the blink of an eye the order she gave to Betty now sits itself in front of her. The burger, fries and pie are all steaming, while her beer bottle has frosty ice crystals all over it, "What is this?" Misty has no choice asking Betty even though her eyes are telling her what she sees is for real.

"Your order Misty. I hope you enjoy it."

Misty's tummy grumbles so loud this time Betty hears it, "My goodness Misty, how long has it been since you've eaten?"

Misty shakes her head so she can stop looking at her order that sits in front of her so she can look at Betty, "Awhile Betty."

"Why?"

"That's a long story Betty and one I don't feel like telling. I hope you don't mind?"

"No Misty, your privacy is yours. I was just concerned."

"Thank you for understanding Betty. If you don't mind can I ask you something?"

"Go ahead Misty."

"Why are you dressed like you're from the late 1960's?"

"That's very simple to answer Misty. The reason I'm dressed like this is because the person you see is indeed from the late 1960's. 1969 in fact."

Misty stands back up and opens up her purse, "Yes you are Betty. When I first set my eyes on you that is just what I thought."

"Do not try to humor me Misty, I'm not crazy."

"I never said you were Betty. But none the less it's for the best if I get going now. How much do I owe you?"

"Nothing Misty. Your order is on the house."

"Thank you Betty, you are very kind. Okay I'm leaving now. It's been very nice meeting you."

"Wait Misty, you don't even want to drink your beer first before you leave?"

Misty looks over at her bottle of beer then back at Betty who's now lighting up a joint. "That's okay Misty if you don't want to drink your beer. Because it looks so good and I'll drink it myself if you don't want it?"

Misty nods her head to Betty and sits back down. She reaches for her beer and opens it up.

She takes a drink and then she reaches out her hand for Betty to hand her, her joint. Betty exhales and jokingly asks, "Are you old enough Misty?"

Misty laughs and takes the joint out of Betty's hand and jokingly says back in response before she takes a toke, "I've been old enough for weed my whole life Betty."

"Well than toke away Misty. In fact you can have that joint, I'll just light up another one." Betty does this and takes a very big toke which chokes her.

Misty laughs almost choking herself, then she's frightened when a second bottle of beer appears in front of her on the counter, "What?"

Betty stops coughing and says, "You didn't think I would let you drink alone? Did you Misty?" Then she opens up her bottle of beer and takes a big thirsty drink from it.

After Betty gets done drinking more of her beer, Misty asks her, "You alright now Betty?"

"Never better Misty."

Both Betty and Misty drink their beers and smoke the rest of their joints in silence. When they get done Misty looks down at her food and is now happily ready to eat it. Betty watches this and says, "Don't eat that Misty, it's cold already."

"I don't mind Betty. Besides it's my fault it's gotten cold. I was hungry but I didn't really feel like eating because I'm so depressed. But thanks to you, your beer and weed I'm feeling a whole lot better now and I'm ready to eat."

Misty reaches down to pick up her burger and it disappears right before she can, "What happened? My food is all gone?"

214

Betty laughs out so hard she has to wipe tears away from her eyes, "Don't worry Misty one new order for you is coming right up."

Misty looks down and her complete order is sitting in front of her again. So instead of freaking out she says, "Cool." And grabs her burger before it can disappear again. Betty walks away to her bedroom so Misty can eat in peace. When she gets back Misty is eating her apple pie, "This apple pie is amazing Betty."

"Thank you Misty. The recipe is from an old friend of mine."

"You're very lucky she gave you her recipe. This friend of yours could sell these pies for herself."

"She's too busy Misty. Out of respect for her recipe, this is the reason why it will be the only kind of apple pie that's ever served inside Eternity's Diner."

"I don't blame you at all Betty. Besides why would you? Your friends apple pie is the very best I've ever tasted."

"Everyone who ever tasted it says the very same thing."

"I believe that Betty. I'm a believer."

"Now after you've finished your apple pie I'd like you to tell me why you were so depressed when you entered my Eternity's Diner?"

"I don't want to bother you Betty."

"It's no bother Misty. It's what I do."

"What is that Betty?"

"I help good people out like you Misty. I help them with one small thing they want or need."

"Well Betty my troubles is a combination of want and need. I want and I need to find my mother's wedding ring so I can wear it for my wedding that's coming up very soon. Like in a week. I can't believe I lost it."

"When is the last time you saw your ring Misty?"

"Three days ago when I took it out of its drawer to look at it. I don't remember putting it back in its drawer. When I did remember it was not in it or anywhere else I could see."

"Alright Misty I'll see what I can do for you. Let me have your address."

Misty looks at Betty and knows she can trust her so she gives her her address and then asks, "Now what Betty?"

"You wait for me to get back out of my room." Betty walks away and enters the control room of her Eternity's Diner as Misty watches her leave in disbelief. Ten minutes later Betty comes out of her control room with a very big smile, "Here you go Misty, now you can get married next week."

Misty takes her ring out of Betty's hand and starts jumping up for joy. Then with the world's biggest smile on her face she gives Betty the thank you hugs of thank you hugs. After this she has to ask, "Betty how did you come to find my ring?"

"Misty this is what you wanted and needed. Be happy that you have it back and leave your question satisfied that it will never be answered."

"Thank you Betty." Misty leaves Betty's Eternity's Diner with tears of joy falling from her eyes. When she's out of the doors, Betty's Eternity's Diner disappears from sight. Misty takes a deep breath and stares deeply at the empty spot that is now in front of her. She drives happily home so she can call Wayne and tell him the great news.

Thus Ends Betty Helps Misty Find Her Missing Ring. This short story was finished at 3:23 PM on April 3rd 2018.

Keith Starblue